HOMESICK *for* EDEN

Giving consideration to the world
God originally prepared for us.

DALE R. MINOR

ISBN 978-1-64569-610-0 (paperback)
ISBN 978-1-64569-611-7 (digital)

Christian Faith Publishing, Inc.
832 Park Avenue
Meadville, PA 16335
www.christianfaithpublishing.com

All scripture references, unless otherwise identified, are taken from the New King James version of the Bible as printed by Holman Bible Publishers (Nashville, Tennessee, 2013).

Printed in the United States of America

CONTENTS

PREFACE

For more than two years, the Lord has had me reading and re-reading Genesis chapters one through three from the Bible. I have written short articles and included some snippets from things I have learned in the process in my earlier book, *His Familiar Voice*. Finally, I think the Lord is working in me to gather my numerous thoughts and conclusions about the Bible's accounts of creation and is driving me to write this volume.

Among the many things I have learned from the story of creation is that it is not just a story about what God did, but it exposes all the Lord intended for mankind and offers relief to our troubled souls. My premise is that the garden of Eden was planted by God specifically to be the dwelling place for man who was created to live eternally. Therefore, the garden God planted would need to provide all that this man and his descendants would need for eternity. Since the Lord Jesus Christ said, "Man does not live by bread alone," this provision would need to be sufficient for all his needs; it would need to nurture him, body, mind, and spirit.

A second premise is that mankind has within him a divine memory, as it were, for the things of Eden. It is our ancestral home, and like many folks today who have a longing to search out the place of their family roots, we have a longing to return to Eden. Sometime and someplace such longings will arise in us and cause a restlessness, the source of which may be elusive, but given due consideration, we may come to realize we are homesick for Eden.

Since the book of Genesis provides only brief descriptions of God's garden, we are left to search elsewhere for clues as to its make-up, and there can be no more reliable source other than the Creator himself and his inerrant word, the Holy Bible. In this book, we will search these scriptures to see what we can learn about the structure of the garden of Eden and why God considered it all necessary.

1

A World Not Our Own

In the novel, *Swiss Family Robinson* by Johann David Wyss, we are given the opportunity to join a family of castaways as they explore, and learn to live, in an alien world. And while this world is neither that which they had left, nor that to which they thought they would go, they learned to live and love the life they have been given with its joys and sorrows, with its blessings and peril.

Such is the life we live, no longer residing in Eden, in the land God prepared for those He created in His own image, but as cast-aways in a foreign land, a place of exile and a land not truly our own. Yet unlike the island created in the mind of Mr. Wyss, the world in which we find ourselves is far less accommodating and becoming increasingly perilous. Indeed, we, its inhabitants, appear to be bent on self-destruction born out of the sinfulness which resulted in our initial exile.

That we often endure hardship is no surprise to believers who accept the biblical story of creation as well as to those who do not; but for the believer, a reason is found in the exile itself. In the book of Genesis, the first three chapters, we are given a description of the world God designed for man as well as a brief account of the failures, the pride and disobedience, which led to the pain and suffering we now experience.

We will get into the specifics of this sin later, but for the moment, let us consider the consequence of the sin. When God confronted Adam over his disobedience, he blamed the woman God had given him; the woman blamed the serpent, Satan, so in Genesis 3:14 we read,

> *So, the Lord God said to the serpent: "Because you have done this, you are cursed more than all the cattle, and more than every beast of the field; on your belly you shall go and you shall eat dust all the days of your life. And I will put enmity between you and the woman, and between your seed and her seed; he shall bruise your head, and you shall bruise his heel.*
>
> *To the woman He said:*
>
> *"I will greatly multiply your sorrow and your conception; in pain you shall bring forth children; your desire shall be for your husband and he shall rule over you."*
>
> *Then to Adam He said,*
>
> *"Because you have heeded the voice of your wife and eaten of the tree of which I commanded you, saying, 'You shall not eat of it': Cursed is the ground for your sake; in toil you shall eat of it all the days of your life. Both thorns and thistles it shall bring forth for you, and you shall eat the herbs of the field. In the sweat of your brow you shall eat bread till you return to the ground, for out of it you were taken; for dust you are, and to dust you shall return."*

In these few verses, within the confines of a couple sentences spoken to these three characters of the story, we are given the seed of every ill known to man and ample proof that we are now living in an alien land; in a land, in which we were not designed to live. So let's review the conditions God identified with life in this alien land; conditions which did not exist in Eden.

First is enmity between Satan and mankind; the root of spiritual warfare and the genesis of much of the mental, physical, and spiritual torment mankind currently endures. Not that God created this satanic confrontation but that he allowed mankind to continue in the bond he willingly formed when he chose alignment with Satan over obedience to God. And it is important for us to acknowledge the generational aspect of this sentence. It has and will affect all generations who walk this earth.

Second is sorrow and pain; specifically, that involving procreation of children which extends beyond the physical pain of childbirth to include the pain and suffering parents often endure as they witness the struggles of their family and particularly if they suffer strained or broken relationships with their children. Also, within this curse is that establishing a hierarchy within the family order which continues to cause struggles in marriages and societies to this day; that which places responsibility for the family to the husband. A requirement too often shirked by the man or usurped by the woman.

To Adam, to mankind, God decreed that the earth would no longer willingly give up its bounty to provide for him and his family apart from hard work and sweat. No longer will he live in a lush garden prepared to provide everything he would ever need with only minimal effort on his part, but that he would have to work for it. He would have to dig in the soil, struggle against the briars and the thistles, and deal with the heat and the cold—with all the elements. This speaks to more than just raising a vegetable garden; it is a metaphor for life in general. No matter the line of work, no matter our means of our livelihood, there will be the need to dig and plant, to cultivate the surroundings; there will be those prickly barriers which spring up to interfere with our plans and dreams, and there will be failures created by unfavorable conditions which prevent our work from bearing fruit. This is life in an alien land.

Finally, God introduced a concept foreign to these, our first parents—death! "In the sweat of your brow you shall eat bread till *you return to the ground,* for out of it you were taken; for dust you are, and *to dust you shall return.*"

We were created immortal. Death was not a part of God's plan for us. It entered into our experience because of sin, for sin is death. It was then; it is now, and it always will be.

Yet there is hope within our exile. *God has not abandoned us!* Even in our banished state, even as we dwell in this foreign land and have become citizens of a world not our own, God, our merciful Father, has not left us as orphans. He has kept His hand on us and continues to encourage us to return to Him, to return to a state of unbroken relationship and constant companionship with Him. And this is grace arising out of His love and mercy.

We see this played out as we study the Old Testament. We see it as God identified Israel as His chosen people. We see it as He prepared Joseph, son of Jacob (Israel), to save his family and build a nation while, yes, in a foreign land. We see it as He delivered these same people, no longer a family but a nation, from bondage and brought them to the land of promise; all the while enduring their obstinate ways, assuring the blessing of his promise in spite of their stiff-necked resistance to Him. And we see it as He preserved a remnant to return from captivity in Babylon to once again build a nation of faithful believers—at least some were faithful.

While this shows that God still loves His people, it falls far short of a return to Eden. God wasn't ready to do that. But it did demonstrate his patience and his compassion for those He calls His own. Even in years of perceived abandonment as during the four hundred years of enslavement in Egypt and seventy years of Babylonian captivity; even in years of silence, such as when He went four hundred years without speaking to the people—without a prophet in Israel; God did not abandon His people but watched over them, preparing them for the time when He would come to visit them in person; in the person of His Son, Jesus Christ our Lord who in turn, when the time was right for His departure, sent the Holy Spirit to be our ready help and guide. This, too, is grace; grace sufficient to teach us how to live in a world in which we were not designed to live and perhaps, for those who can see and believe, raises hope for a return to Eden.

Yes, even after hundreds of generations, we still have within us a longing to go home, to return to the house prepared for us.

We possess an aboriginal memory of our ancestral home, and we are homesick for Eden even as we may not fully understand our yearnings. God knows it. And He wants that as well. Eden is the place God built for us to be in perpetual relationship with Him. It is the garden in which, as the old hymn says, "He walks with me, and talks to me, and tells me I am His own."

Jesus came to make that possible; He came to deliver us from the sin which has enslaved us and exiled us and to bring reconciliation between us and our Lord. He has opened the gates of heaven and become the means by which we may enter into eternal life, that is, to return to the place where death no longer has a hold over us. Is this a new Eden? Let's read on.

Scripture provides us with images of heaven as well as a glimpse into Eden. And while, at first glance, these may be extreme opposites—a gleaming city with streets of gold versus a lush garden—a closer look reveals a common joy; the place where we sit down with the Lord our God and join in His presence and His glory, forever.

However, for now, until Christ returns, we remain aliens residing in a foreign land. And we remain homesick, longing for the Eden which exists in the core of our spirits. Yet it may not be as far from us as we might suppose. If we consider all that we know about Eden, we may find that it is not so far away as we fear. It is not as completely lost to us as we perceive. Indeed, some of us may be closer to Eden than others. A situation which may simultaneously confound and amaze us; while providing evidence that God's grace extends both forward to heaven and back to our roots, to Eden.

To find our Eden, we must first understand the Eden God prepared for His prized creation, mankind. We need to examine the world in which Adam lived and understand how it works and why each element of it is important to our living today and our hopes for the future. There is only one place where we can find this information, and it is from the mouth of the Creator himself. We have to search out the Word of God, the Bible, and to do so, we should begin at the beginning, in the book of Genesis.

Let us now consider the world God prepared for us, beginning even before he formed Adam from the dust of the earth.

2

The Divine Design

The story of creation in the Bible is fascinating though brief. It is amazing in its completeness even as it is lacking in detail. And what may be surprising to many is the reason God created the universe to start with—to provide a home for mankind. Some folks may laugh at such a premise believing that man is just a blip on the scale of universal weight. But as we examine the story of creation, we can readily see that from the beginning God had man in mind. Rather than being an afterthought, a last-ditch spark of creativity in the mind of God, he is His purpose. Rather than being a postscript to the story God was weaving, mankind is its focal point. Indeed, if we limit our reasoning to sheer volume or astrophysical knowledge, the whole earth is but a cosmic speck of dust; but if we consider the story as it is presented and the obvious intent of its author, God, then man becomes its key character and Eden is his home.

But man is not alone in this saga. He lives in the presence of God, enjoys the companionship of God, and owes his existence to God. Actually, the story of creation is autobiographical; it is the story of the beginnings of man born out of God's desire to have a companion made in his own image. Far too often, as we look at the detail provided, we get caught up in questions we can't answer and fail to see and hear the answers which are provided for us. We get overwhelmed by the immensity of universal expanse and questions of time and space and forget the objective of the story. Creation, Genesis 1 and 2, is not a "how-to-book" for building a universe. It is a love story written by the one who is love and who created us to love Him.

Before we even begin with the story, we have to consider its author and hero, God! After all, He was the only one there from the beginning. *"In the beginning God created the heavens and the earth"* (Gen. 1:1). Right away, we may lose some people. But we lose them because they cannot get beyond the fact that we are finite creatures with finite brains and finite understanding, meaning we cannot fully understand the infinity of God. *"Who can understand the mind of God"* (Rom. 11:34). But we are given the means and opportunity to understand the things the Spirit of God reveals to us; means and opportunity provided by the gift of the Holy Spirit himself.

God is spirit and as the scripture says, he was there from the beginning. He was in all three persons of the Holy Trinity: Father, Son, and Holy Spirit. This explains the plurality of Genesis 1:26, "*Then God said, 'Let us make man in our image, according to our likeness.'*" But if God had decided to create a human being, wouldn't the logical first step be to create a world for this man to live in? And if this man was to be created in the image of God and to be a companion of God, wouldn't the place he would live be worthy of God's presence? Wouldn't it be a place of perfection and beauty?

So, from the beginning, God worked to build a world for Adam, a universe. He started with a place described as a "*void, without form, dark and damp*" (see Gen. 1:2). But the Spirit of God was hovering over this indescribable mass which had no life, no purpose until God spoke to it. "*Let there be light,*" and there was light, and God created night and day.

Next, He created a firmament which he called heaven. Don't get confused here. While the sound of the word firmament leads us to think of solid ground, the word actually means the heavens. Even as physically the heavens appear to be mostly air, spiritually, heaven is the source of all solid ground. Let's continue.

And he divided the waters such that there was water both above and below this firmament. This, our story tells us, was the work of the second day of creation. If anyone had been around to observe this, it would have made no sense; its purpose would have been obscure. But He was laying the foundation for the home He was preparing for His greatest creation to come. The third day he looked upon the waters under the heavens and created a divide. He separated the water by creating large areas of dry land which he called earth, and the waters he called seas.

Watch a craftsman, say a potter. He begins with a lump of clay, just a shapeless mass of earth and water. Already he has in mind what he wants to do with it; a vision of the finished product as he starts it spinning on the wheel. The touch of his hands is sufficient to change it slowly and surely. An observer may wonder what he is making and come to first one conclusion then another as the item takes shape. Yet only the craftsman knows when he is through. It has been said the test of a true artist is to know when the work is finished.

Things were looking up, but God was not done. This man he envisioned would need food and shelter. He would need purpose by way of work and inspiration arising from a world of beauty; so God made the earth fruitful. All kinds of grasses and plants and trees, especially trees which would produce seed-yielding fruit which provided food as well as being self-propagating. One can almost imagine God becoming giddy as he added species after species, and this was just the third day.

But if these plants as well as other creatures God had in mind for His world were to live, they would need light. So this was the task for the fourth day; to create lights to rule both the day and the night. He set the sun in place to rule the day and the moon, the night. He also created stars to assist the moon and become guiding lights for man.

But then God really got busy. His creative juices were really flowing; as on the fifth day, He created fish and other creatures to live in the seas. Then He made birds to fill the sky, perhaps just to cause his earthbound creatures to occasionally look upward to the heavens. And if that wasn't enough, He began the sixth day be creating all kinds of living creatures, cattle and creeping things and beasts of the earth. Then God surveyed all He had made, and it was good! And yet His work wasn't done.

Finally, the preparatory work was completed. It was time for the objective of His work; man, the one He would call Adam and his mate, Eve. Genesis 1:27,

> *"So, God created man in His own image; in the image of God He created him, male and female He created them."*

In the second account of creation in Genesis 2:21–23, we find the more popular story of the creation of Eve. How God took a rib out of Adam's' side and formed Eve which perhaps provides more detail, but the important part of the story is that God created man in His own image, with His own nature, for the purpose of being His own faithful companion and placed him in the garden; the world He had created especially for him.

There are a couple key details provided here which often are overlooked or dismissed but are really important for our understanding of who we are and for our eternal relationship with the Lord. First of all, it has already been stated that God is spirit. There can be no doubt from the text of Genesis 1 that God's primary goal was the creation of man, *in his image!* If God is spirit and we are made in His image, does this not mean that we are spirit beings at our core? In the first part of the twentieth century, French Jesuit paleontologist, biologist, and philosopher; Pierre Teilhard de Chardin wrote, "We are not physical beings having a spiritual experience; we are spiritual beings having a physical experience." This is further affirmed in scripture as in Genesis 2:7,

> *"And the Lord formed man of the dust of the ground and breathed into his nostrils the breath of life; and man became a living being."*

This is important in that even as God had formed the man from the dust of the earth; from the basic elements of the world he had formed, it remained just a lump of clay until God breathed life into him. His life, the breath of God, His own life-giving spirit was breathed into mankind so that he might live.

God had created other living creatures. Swimming creatures, flying creatures, four-legged, two-legged, creeping and crawling creatures and in no place is it indicated that God breathed His spirit into them. He blessed these and instructed them to be fruitful and multiply, but he did not breathe true life into them. Only in man and for man did God impart the gift of His own breath, and why? To give him His spirit and complete the process of making him in His image.

So God had established the universe, the totality of substance and space constructed for man to live, and it was huge! Why so vast? Only God knows, but perhaps its primary purpose is to cause man to look up, to search out that firmament, God's heavenly home; to allow him to discover and begin to understand the immensity of God. In any regard, we have to assume it is all necessary even as the reasoning may now be and always remain obscure. For sure, it was much too large for this creature's comfort. Even this rock, the earth, was far beyond the scope of this man's reach or vision. So be it. God took care of that as well. Genesis 2:8,

> "The Lord *God planted a garden* (in Greek, *paradeisos*) eastward in Eden, and *there He put the man He had formed.* And out of the ground the Lord made every tree grow that is pleasant to the eye and good for food. The tree of life was also in the midst of the garden, and the tree of the knowledge of good and evil."

We also know that there was plenty of water there. Verses ten through fourteen tell us that a river ran out from Eden sufficient to split into four riverheads; only one still known by the name given it in Genesis, the Euphrates. (Efforts to locate Eden in relationship to these rivers are confounded by the fact that rivers change their courses over time, and events, especially the great flood survived only by Noah and his family, would have greatly altered the landscape and courses of such rivers.)

So man had everything he would need food, water, shelter, a place to work. (God put Adam in the garden to tend it.) Further, while, as previously mentioned and we will discover again and again, a lot of detail we might like to have seen or heard is missing from this story. It was important to God and for the life and health of mankind to mention that He also provided things that were pleasant to the eye. This seems to indicate that we are designed to recognize and appreciate beautiful things for what they are, and that they are necessary for our well-being. Most of all, the beauty of the earth helps us to visualize the unfathomable beauty of being in the presence of the Creator, in the presence of God!

While Genesis 2:9 indicates there were numerous types of trees, the story focuses on two. The tree of life and that of the knowledge of good and evil. The second one bore forbidden fruit; the first provided eternal life. The second, God said, would bring death, the first, life. Thus, those who eat of these trees would have far reaching and exact opposite experiences. Of course, chapter 3 of Genesis tells us what happened to Adam and Eve and the future for mankind. There we learn how, after being persuaded by a sly and evil serpent, Eve first then Adam ate from this tree of the knowledge of good and evil and thus God banished them from Eden. This act of disobedience, choosing their way over God's way, was tantamount to setting themselves up as their own gods and established them in a state of rebellion against God. Thus, if they then ate of the tree of life, this fallen condition would continue for eternity. God could not let that happen. They were expelled from the garden and permanently banished from ever returning. There were other consequences which have already been mentioned and which will be discussed as we go on.

Now, there has been a lot written about the expanse of time provided in the story of creation, that defined as six days. Astrophysicists speak of the creation of the universe in terms of hundreds of billions of years and are learning daily how this universe is much larger than anyone ever imagined. After all, how do you measure infinity?

Some claim that the word, "day," in the accounts did not mean a twenty-four-hour day as we know it. They may point to the fact that the sun wasn't even set in the sky until the fourth day. However, it is also true that the omniscient, omnipotent God we worship, He who has the power to create the universe and all that is in it, can certainly do it in the time of His choosing even with the snap of his finger. (Would not the snap of God's finger create a big bang?) But there has been very little written about the hours, days, or years Adam and Eve spent in the garden. One can read through Genesis chapters one through three and get the idea that they got up their first morning together and started a conversation with the serpent. But sometimes we have to read between the lines.

For sure, we have to be careful. We don't want to get ourselves into the position of violating the warnings we are given about adding to or subtracting from the Scriptures; and even as the following requires some assumptions, they are assumptions based upon Scripture. And the first assumption is that God's human experience was not a failure. It's not a failure because it isn't over, and God has known from the beginning what is needed and how it turns out. Second, indications are that Adam and Eve enjoyed some time in the presence of God before violating his command. They walked with Him and talked with Him in the garden. They had enough experience with Him to recognize the sound of his steps walking in the garden, and they definitely knew the sound of His voice. They had sufficient experience with God to know who He is and to have enjoyed His presence. They had sufficient experience with Him to know He would not be happy with their disobedience as evidenced by the fact they tried to hide from Him.

We can assume that such detail has been omitted from the story God wrote because it really isn't important for us to know. Just as God demanded of Adam, there are certain things we are to accept by faith without knowing all the whys and wheres. What does seem to be important is that God prepared a perfect world for Adam and Eve; one that would provide all they would ever need, and what later perceptive men would describe as inalienable rights like life, liberty, and the pursuit of happiness. There is sufficient evidence that Adam and

Eve enjoyed some time living in this arrangement and had become comfortable in it.

Perhaps this is what attracted Satan, the fallen angel, to enter the serpent and become the tempter of God's chosen. If Satan's base intent is to be like God, then his primary goal would to be to entice God's people to doubt Him, to stray from Him, to rebel against Him, and to deny Him. Most of all He needed those made in God's image to deny their creator and follow him.

To this end he found that the only tools he would ever need are lies, deception, innuendo, and distortion. He used these on Adam and Eve, and He has used them on every person called by God ever since. Satan himself has no power to cause us to do anything, only the power of persuasion. He needs us to cooperate with him, and we have learned to do this quite effectively.

God had a divine purpose for all of creation, and it began with His design and intent for mankind; the one creature endowed with His own likeness, His own nature, His own spirit, and with the ability to reside in perfect harmony with him for perpetuity. Along with the pleasing atmosphere and divine companionship, God also provided for the physical needs of mankind. It began with the garden. As it says in Genesis 2:9,

> *"Out of the ground the Lord God made every tree grow that is pleasant to the sight and good for food."*

Since Jesus would, in Matthew 4:4, quote from Deuteronomy 8:3 to remind us that *"man shall not live by bread alone but by every word that proceeds from the mouth of God."* It is obvious that "food" does not mean only protein and carbohydrates. It means all that sustains us body, mind, and spirit. Therefore, we should spend some time learning what kinds of food the Lord provided for mankind. What were the nutrients the Lord intended to help us live in His presence forever? And perhaps even more important, we must answer the question, "Are such nutrients available to us yet today?"

3

Two Trees in a Grove

Genesis 2 tells us that God placed Adam and Eve in a garden. It says that the Lord provided every type of tree needed for man's pleasure and which was good for food. But it tells us very little about these trees—except for two. Therefore, we can assume that these two were the most important of them all. An assumption borne out as we continue to read Genesis 3 and the remainder of Holy Scripture. But they weren't the only trees in the garden. There were other trees growing there which provided various fruits to eat as well as some whose purpose was to enhance the beauty of man's world. It seems that there was at least a grove, if not an immense forest, of trees. These we will deal with later, but for now, let us consider the two that God tells us the most about.

The tree most discussed in chapters two and three of Genesis is the *tree of the knowledge of good and evil.* It, along with *the tree of life,* was in the midst of the garden. This implies that they were handy to Adam and Eve; they were nearby. God told Adam that he could eat from every tree which bore fruit except for one, the one He called the tree of the knowledge of good and evil. Don't eat from that tree; God warned. Paraphrasing, God said, "That fruit is poisonous. It will kill you. Eat that fruit and you will die" (Gen. 2:16–17)! This seems like a straight forward and fair warning.

Artist and story tellers of our day like to portray this tree as that bearing an apple. In fact, this is an ancient image. The lump in a man's throat is called his "Adam's apple" in reference to this perception. But an apple is the fruit of an apple tree. God declared this tree to be that of the *knowledge* of good and evil. Thus, its fruit is not food for the stomach but stimulants for the mind. Its effects were far more dangerous than an upset stomach or diarrhea. It poisoned the mind; perhaps made him delirious; at very least, put him in a state of mental confusion, an easy prey for Satan. But first, the serpent had to entice Adam to eat of this fruit, and he chose Eve to take the first bite.

A logical question is why God would have planted such a tree in the first place. The answer lies in the decision God made to give man free will. God's desire is that man would love Him as He himself loves us. Jesus declared this to be the first and great commandment that, *"We love the Lord our God with all our heart, with all our soul, and with all our mind"* (Matt. 22:36). But love exists only in the freedom to choose or reject. Jesus also said, *"If you love me, keep my commandments"* (John 14:15). This is not an attempt to pull out of us a feeble declaration of love, but a truth spoken concerning the nature of God's commandments; that they are food for our hearts and our minds and our souls. They are the *"words that proceed from the mouth of God"* (Matt. 4:4). Words which Jesus says are even more important than food for our stomachs.

Was this just a test? An enticement arranged by God to entrap Adam into disobedience? Such a test would seem to be counter to God's nature and his purpose for creating man in the first place. The whole structure of the garden was for the care, nurture, and pleasure of mankind. Perhaps the primary purpose of the tree was to establish some boundaries and to help Adam know and understand how good life in the garden really was. It is true for all of us that we need trials in order to appreciate the blessings. We need sorrows in order to understand the joy. Every parent has had to deal with their toddler testing the boundaries we set for them. All we need to do is to declare a certain place or object off limits, and it becomes a siren call for them to test it. Is this a part of our created human nature, or of the nature we acquired by virtue of the fall of man?

However, we may look at it; the basic truth is that the existence of this tree of the knowledge of good and evil came out of the infinite wisdom of God. If we believe in God, if we believe the opening words of His book, "In the beginning God," then we accept the fact that in spite of its negative impact upon the occupants of the garden, the Lord, the Creator of the universe deemed it necessary that this tree exist. We can conjecture all we want as to what would have happened if this tree had not existed, or if the serpent had not been successful in his efforts to lure mankind into disobedience to God, but we have to acknowledge this one basic fact; it wouldn't matter if the tree was there or not if Adam and Eve had not disobeyed God's direct order.

There is a condition of man's character which causes us to question most things. We need to see proof that what we are told is true. It's like seeing a sign that says, "Wet Paint" and having to touch the paint to see if it is in fact uncured. Sometimes this trait serves us well, but more often than not, it leads to bad results. Satan certainly uses this trait to our disadvantage. He constantly tells us that the things we have been told for our benefit are not that important.

> "'*Did God really tell you that if you eat from that tree you will die? You will not surely die!'* the serpent told them. '*For God knows that if you eat it your eyes will be opened and you will be like God, knowing good from evil'*" (Gen. 3:4).

Not only did the serpent challenge God's warning of the consequence of any disobedience, but he offered a substitute reason for why God did not want them to eat of this tree, *"Because it will make you like God."* It will make you equal to God; it will elevate your status; all these things which pique the interest of man, Satan offered in one brief statement. "Listen to me, follow me," he said, "and I will satisfy your every need. I will give you worldly possessions, and I will give you status."

The deceptions which Satan used on Adam and Eve are summed up in 1 John 2:16 as, *"The lust of the flesh, the lust of the eyes, and the pride of life."* And since they worked so well on God's chosen creation, he would use these same enticements on Jesus in the wilderness temptations as described in Matthew chapter 4. But Jesus had the strength to resist the temptations and to order Satan out of his sight.

We, on the other hand, continue to listen to Satan's lies. We are prone to fall victim to these same three enticements; in fact, many of us eagerly seek them out. We live as if we have a tree of the knowledge of good and evil in our own backyards, and we eat of its fruit daily. And we, like our first parents, will suffer the consequence for our disobedience; the consequence of sin, of the curse of life outside the garden, death and alienation from God, except as we are saved by the blood of Christ.

But let's look further, God told Adam that if he ate of this tree he would die. Satan denied that statement. Obviously, from the fact that we are here, Adam and Eve did not die immediately. They lived to bear sons and daughters to begin the process of populating the world. Genesis 5:5 tells us that Adam lived 930 years. Their first two sons, Cain and Abel, lived to be adults before Cain murdered his brother. This was the first human death as far as we know. It was the death of a fruit of Adam's seed. And after the death of Abel, Adam sired another son, Seth; this when he was 130 years old, and after that, he had other sons and daughters. Death would come to Adam; God's promises are sure. But it would take a while. We could even say that Adam died a slow death.

As we read on, we discover there were additional consequences of the sin of Adam to be endured. These are summarized under the heading of the curse placed upon mankind and upon the world in which he would now live. Since these affect the world we live in and, apart from the saving grace of Jesus we still endure, it is advisable that we understand their details. Let's review Genesis 3:14–19.

> *So, the Lord said to the serpent: "Because you have done this, you are cursed more than all the cat-*

> *tle, and more than every beast of the field; on your belly you shall go, and you shall eat dust all the days of your life. And I will put enmity between you and the woman, and between your seed and her seed; He shall bruise your head, and you shall bruise His heel."*

Is there any creature on earth which brings more fright, anxiety, immediate revulsion in most of us, except for a serpent? The mere sight of even a small harmless snake creates a desire in us to flee or to immediately kill the snake. But there is a subtle but important detail in verse 15 which needs to be noted. The concluding sentence of the curse placed upon the serpent says, "*He shall bruise your head and you shall bruise His heel.*" The He and His in this sentence are capitalized indicating deity. And theologically, we understand that even then, by speaking of the seed of the woman, God was looking ahead to the Savior; He was projecting the Promised One, the Christ who would come to defeat Satan. The word "seed" is used throughout the Bible as a messianic term. And consider the detail of the ongoing battle between the seed of the woman and that of the serpent. *"You shall bruise His heel;"* that is, you will be able to inflict pain and suffering; you may even be able to temporarily cripple, but *"He shall bruise your head!"* That is a death blow. It is the end of the battle, and it will come. This says that the enemy will strike at us, but his bite will not be terminal. But when the Savior, born of a woman, strikes the head of the serpent, it is a fatal blow.

Continuing with the curse, verse 16.

> *"To the woman He said, 'I will greatly multiply your sorrow and your conception; in pain you shall bring forth children; your desire shall be for your husband. And he shall rule over you.'"*

Not only, in this brief description of the curse placed upon Eve, do we see how God has taken a moment of intense joy, an event identifying the basic purpose of woman, a moment when she is provided the object and opportunity for the most intense love of her life and inflicted it with pain; but that He has also established what our generation has tabbed "the battle of the sexes." *"Your desire will be for your husband, and he shall rule over you."* We say this differently, but it means the same, "You will try to dominate your husband, and he will attempt to control you." From life in the garden in which there was mutual respect and appreciation for the roles each had in their union, the curse has now placed them in an adversarial relationship. This curse has to be broken!

Finally, this brings to the portion of the curse relating to Adam. Beginning at verse 17; then to Adam He said,

> *"Because you have heeded the voice of your wife and have eaten from the tree of which I commanded you, saying, 'you shall not eat of it'; cursed is the ground for your sake,* (or because of you); *In toil you shall eat of it all the days of your life. Both thorns and thistles it shall bring forth for you, and you shall eat the herb of the field. In the sweat of your face you shall eat bread till you return to the ground, for out of it you were taken; for dust you are and to dust you shall return."*

There is a lot in this passage. Perhaps it needs to be stated here the reason why this is primarily Adam's sin. Why not Eve's sin? Or that of the serpent? That was Adam's viewpoint when confronted by God for their sin. He played that blame game as we read in Genesis 3:11b–13,

> *"And He* (God) *asked, 'Have you eaten from the tree of which I commanded you that you should not eat?' Then the man said, 'the woman whom You gave to be with me, she gave me of the tree and I ate.'"*

Not only had Adam blamed Eve, but he implied the real fault was God's for giving him the woman. The woman, in turn, blamed the serpent.

But neither of these arguments hold water. To whom did God give instructions concerning life in the garden? It was Adam. In Genesis 2:16, we find;

> *"And the Lord God commanded the man, saying, 'Of every tree of the garden you may freely eat; but of the tree of the knowledge of good and evil you shall not eat, for in the day you shall eat of it you shall surely die.'"*

Not only was this spoken specifically to Adam, it was spoken *before Eve was created.* It was not until verses eighteen to twenty-four that we learn of God's decision to provide a companion for Adam.

But equally important is what God says about this companion. *"It is not good for man to be alone; I will make him a helper* comparable *to him."* This statement carries two truths: 1) that this woman was not a lower-class creature but is indeed equal to Adam; and 2) that God charged Adam with looking after her. It is not about equality; it is about defining the roles each was to have. Eve was to be his helper, not his servant nor his boss. Helper means one who aids, assists, cooperates with, rather than one who serves. Adam, not Eve, was given the responsibility for heeding God's instruction for life in the garden; therefore, it was Adam's sin for not protecting his mate from the temptation. Adam left his wife vulnerable and then seeing that she ate the forbidden fruit and did not immediately drop dead, joined her in the sin.

So far, we have heard the directive from the mouth of God concerning the punishment He was meting out to Adam and Eve, but we have not answered the question concerning their exile from the garden. That answer is found in Genesis 3:22.

"Then the Lord God said, 'Behold, the man has become like one of Us, to know good and evil.'" Note, it does not say "to know good *from* evil," nor does it say to "know *about* good and evil," but that he *knows* both; they are both within him. *"And now, lest he put out his hand and take also from the* tree of life, *and eat, and live forever—*

therefore the Lord God sent him out from the garden of Eden to till the ground from which he was taken."

It is interesting in all the intrigue of this drama, that God just didn't choose to uproot this tree of life. He not only chose to leave it in the center of the garden, but He posted a guard to prevent man from returning to it. Genesis 3:24, the last verse describing life in the garden of Eden says,

> *"So, He drove out the man, and He placed cherubim at the east of the garden of Eden, and a flaming sword which turned every way. To guard the way to the tree of life."*

Having succumbed to temptation, having been disobedient to God, the next great danger was that man would also eat of the tree of life and become immortal and would live forever in his sin. While we fully understand man's exile from the garden of Eden to be a serious matter, we can also take heart in that allowing the *tree of life* to grow on is an act of mercy on the part of God. By removing man from access to the tree of life in the garden, He placed him in position to become the beneficiary of the Savior who would come to offer eternal life for those who would turn their hearts to Him.

This provides a measure of hope, the opportunity of the day to come when we will regain access to the tree of life. Indeed, in Revelation 22, in John's vision of the New Jerusalem, he speaks of the river of water which flows out from the throne of God, and says in verse 2, *"And on either side of the river, was* the tree of life, *which bore twelve fruits, each tree yielding its fruit every month."*

We will look deeper into what Scripture tells us about this tree in the next chapter.

4

The Tree of Life

The feature second most discussed in the story of creation and the fall of man is the tree of life, but this does not mean it is second in importance. Instead, from God's actions in restricting access by the exiled offenders, we can see that this tree is most important to the story and as we will learn, to the future of mankind.

In the previous chapters, we disclosed God's own words that the purpose of this tree was immortality. It was stated that if man would eat of the fruit of this tree, he would live forever. (Gen. 3:22) But as we examine the presence of this tree and its lasting effects in the minds of men, we will see that it involves more than longevity; it is also about quality of life. Jesus himself declared this in the prayer He prayed with his disciples immediately before going out to the garden of Gethsemane as in John 17:3;

> *"(Father,)...this is eternal life, that they* (believers) *may know You, the only true God, and Jesus Christ whom you have sent."*

The tree of life is symbolic of our bond with God in Christ Jesus, for He alone provides purpose to our living; it is in Him that quality of life is secured.

Before we can understand the importance of this tree, we first have to understand the meaning of life as God intended it to be. The beginning chapters of this book devoted considerable space impressing upon the reader the impact of God's decision to make man in his image, and we have learned that the process God used was unique; that he formed man from the dust of the earth, but he remained nothing more than a lump of clay until God breathed life into him.

> *"And the Lord God formed man out of the dust of the ground, and breathed into his nostrils the breath of life, and man became a living being"* (Gen. 2:7).

There is no indication that God so breathed life into any other of the living creatures he made. This was reserved for man because the breath given to man was the Spirit of God. God breathed His own spirit into man which gave him life and imparted within him His own nature or image which, of course, was the Creator's stated intent for this creature. Therefore, when we talk about life as it relates to the man God created, it has to be life encased within and dependent upon the Spirit of God.

The nature of this spirit is not fully revealed in Genesis. But it is revealed in the rest of God's story, the Holy Scriptures, particularly in the Gospels of Jesus Christ. As we read of God's interaction with man throughout the ages, we become privy to the heart of God and thus to the nature of God. And it is the expressed invitation, no, more of a commandment, that we seek the Lord and submit to him.

> *"Therefore, submit to God. Resist the devil and he will flee from you. Draw near to God and He will draw near to you. Cleanse your hands, you sinners; and purify your hearts, you double minded"* (James 4:7–8).

This is a call to align our hearts with that of the Lord; it is a call to live in the image he has given us.

Now, as to the fruit of the tree of life and its eternal gift, let's return to the garden of Eden as it was created. Here again, we are confronted with a conundrum. Why was it necessary for God to provide this tree of life? As we have seen, he planted a whole grove of trees, perhaps even a large forest, with each tree having as its purpose to be pleasing to the eye or good for food. If God wanted man to be immortal, why not just establish immortality within him? Why was it necessary to require that he eat the fruit of this particular tree to gain what God wanted him to have from the beginning?

The answer rests in both the nature of this tree as well as in the affirmation of God's decision to provide choices for man. That is, if we are to be the people God designed us to be, if we are to abound in a love relationship with Him, we have to have the freedom to choose or reject. This extends to the tree of life. God has given us an option, life or death; and He has invited us to choose life. But it remains our choice. As Moses was beginning his final address to the nation of Israel, he spoke these words;

> *See, I have set before you today, life and good, death and evil, in that I command you today to love the Lord your God, to walk in His ways, and to keep his commandments, His statutes, and His judgments, that you may live and multiply; and the Lord your God will bless you in the land which you go in to possess.* (Deut. 30:15–16)

We have been given this gift of free choice; it is both a blessing and a curse. A blessing in that it provides the opportunity and means to express our devotion to God; a curse in that it requires a conscious decision on our part to choose rightly. Since our first parents Adam and Eve chose wrongly, they chose the tree of the knowledge of good and evil and consequently were banned from access to the tree of life, we don't really know what would have happened if they had eaten from this tree—or do we?

If we are to understand the nature of this tree, we have to keep in mind its purpose. It's all about life in God's kingdom; it's about eternal life! Let's look further into scripture. The next time we hear the term, "tree of life" is in the book of Proverbs in King Solomon's writings concerning the wisdom of God. The subject of biblical wisdom is a study within itself and is often difficult to understand particularly as it seems to take on different meanings within the changing cultures of the Old Testament and as we move into the New. The common worldly concept of wisdom is the ability to use intelligence, knowledge, understanding, etc. effectively to come to a right decision; to what is often referred to as common sense. (Although there is ample evidence to suggest it isn't all that common)

Biblical wisdom emanates from the mind of God. It thrives in our desire to know the mind of God while, at the same time, being faithful and submissive to His will. Even as scripture states that we cannot fully know the mind of God, it is true that He reveals to us what He will, and what he wills is sufficient for us to maintain a strong and healthy relationship with Him.

Proverbs 9:10 declares,

> *"The fear of the Lord is the beginning of knowledge, and the knowledge of the Holy One is understanding."*

Fear, meaning reverence and awe, is a healthy respect for the word of God and such reverence demands of us submissive hearts and humble obedience (see also Prov. 1:7). Knowledge means more than intellectual insight; it involves the heart—the meshing of our spirit with His.

Again, we know we cannot fully understand the mind of God, but we are granted access to facets of it which are important to our life and living. Through scripture, certain windows are opened into the inner thoughts of God sufficient for us to exercise wisdom, that is, to make right and godly choices in our lives.

As to how this relates to the tree of life, let's consider the references encased within the book of Proverbs. First is Proverbs 3:13–18. (Note the feminine pronouns speak of wisdom.)

> *Happy is the man who finds wisdom, and the man who gains understanding; for her proceeds are better than the profits of silver, and her gain than fine gold. She is more precious than rubies, and all things you may desire cannot compare with her. Length of days is in her right hand, in her left hand are riches and honor. Her ways are ways of pleasantness, and all her paths are peace. She is* a tree of life *to those who take hold of her, and happy are all who retain her.*

This paragraph gives testimony that wisdom, like the tree of life, provides all the things we will need for good and right living and *for longevity of life;* and it speaks the truth that there is no earthly benefit which can compare to the knowledge of God and life in a healthy relationship with Him. The tree of life, in this context, exists in our obedience to God.

There are three more references to the tree of life in Proverbs in 11:30, *"The tree of righteousness is a* tree of life." In 13:12, *"Hope deferred makes the heart sick, but when the desire comes, it is* a tree of life" (the desire meaning the hope for a return to Eden); then in 15:4, *"A wholesome (or gentle) tongue is* a tree of life, *but perverseness in it breaks the spirit."* When we have the name of Jesus always on our lips, it is difficult for us to speak hurtful words to those we are called to love.

As we move into the New Testament, wisdom is recognized in the person of Jesus Christ. In such scriptures as Matthew 13:54 we hear such acclamation as,

> *"Where did this Man get this wisdom and these mighty works? Is this not the carpenter's son? Is his mother not called Mary?"*

The question of His wisdom came with acknowledgement that Jesus spoke, not by His own knowledge and strength but with the power and authority of God the Father.

And in Luke 11:29–31, speaking to the demands of the people for a sign from heaven testifying that Jesus is who He says he is, Jesus says,

> *This is an evil generation. It seeks a sign, and no sign will be given to it except the sign of Jonah the prophet. For as Jonah became a sign to the Ninevites, so also the Son of Man will be to this generation. The queen of the South will rise up in judgment with this generation and condemn them, for she came from the ends of the earth to hear the wisdom of Solomon; and indeed, a greater than Solomon is here.*

The sign of Jonah refers to his being a prophet sent on a mission to the great city of Nineveh for the purpose of proclaiming the Lord's condemnation of them and to urge them to repent of their wicked ways and the "Queen of the South" refers to the gentile queen of Sheba who sought out the wisdom of Solomon. This passage confesses that Jesus is greater than any who proclaimed God's word in former days. His wisdom surpasses even the best of these.

In 1 Corinthians 2, Saint Paul makes the strong case for Christ attesting that the wisdom of God which is hidden from men has been revealed in the person of Jesus Christ. He proclaims that, in the power of the Holy Spirit, this knowledge is released in mankind. 1 Corinthians 2:14–16 states;

> *The natural man does not receive the things of the Spirit of God, for they are foolishness to him; nor can he know them, because they are spiritually discerned. But he who is spiritual judges all things, yet he himself is rightly judged by no one. For who has known the mind of the Lord that he may instruct Him? But we have the mind of Christ.*

How can Paul claim to have the mind of Christ? The same way we can; through the power of the Holy Spirit who reveals Him to us in the Gospels, in the testimony of witnesses, through revelation, and by our personal experiences with Him.

To summarize, as we search for the tree of life, we find it in the mind of God in what Solomon described as the wisdom of God. Then as we dig further to uncover the wisdom of God, we find Him manifest in the person of Jesus Christ. This in turn begs us to ask the question, *"Is Jesus Christ the tree of life?"*

To answer that question, it might be best to go to the end of the book and work backward. For it is the book of the Revelation of Jesus Christ that we next find testimony relating to the tree of life. Not only is it in the final book of The Bible, but we are called to the last chapter, chapter 22. The previous chapter describes John's vision of the new Jerusalem, the heavenly city, and the throne of God; but as we begin chapter 22, John writes,

> *And he showed me a pure river of water of life, clear as crystal, proceeding from the throne of God and of the Lamb. In the middle of its street, and on either side of the river, was* the tree of life, *which bore twelve fruits,* each tree *yielding its fruit every month. The leaves of the tree were for the healing of the nations, and there shall be no more curse*

This description of the tree leaves us puzzled over precisely what John had seen in his vision. Was this one tree or twelve trees? Maybe it was a huge tree with twelve trunks coming off a common root base? Or more likely, it was an immense tree sitting in the middle of the river with its branches overhanging both banks? It really doesn't matter. What matters is that it draws its strength from the river that flows out from the throne of God. What matters is that the one who eats of the fruit of this tree is drinking the pure water of life sucked up by the roots of this tree of life. It testifies that God has not forgotten Eden nor changed His mind as to the benefits this tree provides for mankind. It provides everything man will need for eternity. Let's look further to discover what that is.

In verse 12, begins Jesus's final promise to the churches and to us.

"Behold, I am coming quickly, and My reward is with Me, to give to everyone according to his work. I am the Alpha and the Omega, the Beginning and the End, the First and the Last." Then John continues, verse14, *"Blessed are those who do His commandments, that they may have* the tree of life, *and may enter through the gates into the city."* Some texts say, "Blessed are they who wash their robes, *that they may have* the right *to* the tree of life."

This then calls us back to Revelation 7:14, describing those who have been made worthy to sit before the throne of God. *"These are the ones who came out of the great tribulation and washed their robes and made them white in the blood of the Lamb."* Therefore, our worthiness before God, our righteousness, is dependent upon the blood of Christ. It is the blood of Christ which cleanses away the dirtiness of our sin and makes us worthy to eat of *the tree of life.*

A second element of the detail John provides for the tree of life in his vision of heaven is that *the leaves of the tree were for the healing of nations.* Healing from what? From the curse God placed upon man as the result of the fall. Understand, the curse pronounced as the result of Adam's sin was not on man only but upon the whole earth, and its effect is tremendous. It was far beyond what anyone in those first days and years could have imagined. Even before God had previously observed the depravity of man and decided to eliminate all He had created by flooding the whole earth, (Genesis 6 and 7) the capacity for man to sin was beyond imagination, and all evidence is that it hasn't gotten any better. In fact, we seem to have gotten really good at inventing new expressions of sin. Yet Christ shed His blood as atonement for our sins and restored us to righteousness in His sight.

The third and most important element to the tree of life as revealed in John's vision is eternal life. Revelation 2:7 promises to the church at Ephesus, to those Jesus charged to have departed from their first love, that those who will repent and return quickly to Him.

> "*To him who overcomes I will give* (the right) *to eat of* the tree of life *which is in the midst of the Paradise of God.*"

Note the wording, "*him who overcomes*" means those who have overcome the effects of their sin; it is the one who by faith in Jesus Christ overcomes the pull of the world and the temptations of Satan. We have chosen to insert the words, "the right," as per Revelation 22:14 to reinforce the fact that access to this tree is a gift. Hear again from the Apostle John.

> *"For whatever is born of God overcomes the world. And this is the victory that has overcome the world—our faith. Who is he who overcomes the world, but he who believes that Jesus is the Son of God"* (1 John 5:4–5)?

It is strictly due to the grace of God and His love for us; it is through the work of His Son, Jesus Christ our Lord, and it is by the power of the Holy Spirit that we can change our wicked ways and submit our lives, turning our hearts over to Him.

So again, is the tree of life Jesus, or *is Jesus the tree of life?* We have to emphatically say, "No!" It's no because of who Jesus is—God himself. As such, He was there when the garden was created and He was party to the populating of it. John 1:1–4,14,

> *In the beginning was the Word, and the Word was with God, and the Word was God. He was in the beginning with God. All things were made through Him, and without Him nothing was made that was made. In Him was life, and the life was the light of men… And the Word became flesh and dwelt among us, and we beheld His glory, the glory as of the only begotten of the Father, full of grace and truth.*

This is Jesus; He is one with the Father and is co-creator with Him. While God is all-powerful and can do what he likes, by definition, He cannot be both Creator and the created. Therefore, the tree of life, a created entity within the garden of Eden, is not Jesus;

however, the tree of life is a precursor to Jesus. It was planted to give mankind the opportunity to fulfill God's desire of eternal life for His chosen creature; a purpose which was passed to Jesus and is fulfilled as we submit to Him and become partakers of His heavenly grace.

Consider some of the things Jesus says about himself. In the Gospel of John, there are seven statements of Jesus beginning with the words "I am." An examination of five of these provides an interesting parallel with what we have learned about the tree of life.

1. John 6:35, *"I am the bread of life. He who comes to Me shall never hunger, and he who believes in Me shall never thirst."*

This speaks to a hunger and thirst separate from our bodily needs and encompasses all things spiritual and eternal, including our longing to return to Eden.

2. John 14:6, *"I am the way, the truth, and the life. No one comes to the father except through Me."*

Jesus is the means to a life which can only grow and flourish in the presence of Almighty God.

3. John 10:11, *"I am the good shepherd. The good shepherd gives His life for the sheep."*

These words were spoken preliminary to Christ's sacrifice for the souls of men, an event providing the ultimate testimony of God's love for us.

4. John 8:12, *"I am the light of the world. He who follows Me shall not walk in darkness but have the light of life."*

The comparison of light and darkness in the gospels provides a powerful image of the vast differences in the lives of those who walk with the Lord as compared to those who follow the ways of the world.

And then number 5. John 11:25, *"I am the resurrection and the life. He who believes in Me, though He may die, he shall live. And he who lives and believes in Me shall never die."*

These and other examples from scripture provide sufficient evidence of the eternal power within the tree of life and its connection to Jesus Christ; a connection designed by the one true God who knew from the beginning that mankind would need a Savior. In the beginning, God planted a tree with the capacity for providing eternal life within the scope of Eden. In his great mercy, He also has given us Jesus and a new tree of life in His new paradise in the realm of heaven.

Another way of looking at this is to compare the tree of life in Genesis to that in Revelation. One effect of being exiled from Eden was that mankind was cut off from his continual fellowship with God. He no longer walked with Him and talked with Him. Granted, through God's intervention, through prophets, kings, and priests, mankind learned to communicate with God but remained unable to enter into the deeply personal and intimate relationship which existed in Eden.

After Jesus ascended into heaven and sent the Holy Spirit to us, a measure of that intimacy became available, but it remains somewhat anemic in us. Anemic because of the worldly interference in the hearts and minds of men. By the resurrection of Christ, in His promise that believers will be raised as He has been raised, we will enter into heaven to dwell in the shadow of the tree of life for perpetuity.

Adam forfeited access to the tree of life in the garden of Eden. Having been exiled from Eden, man was prevented from returning to his original home; however, his expulsion did not cut mankind off from the hope of salvation. But, as God took away what he had given, to survive, His favorite of creation would need assistance in another form. Such assistance came when God, in His timing, gave us Jesus, the author and finisher of our faith. He would open the way to the heavens and call us into His presence as He sits on the throne, feeding us with the fruit from the renewed and greater tree of life.

5

THE EDEN DIET

So far, we have examined the makeup of Eden as provided in the story of Creation and sought out details of the two specific trees identified in Genesis chapter 2. But we also stated that there were more trees in the garden; those not specifically named. As a refresher, let's read again Genesis 2:8–9:

> *"The Lord God planted a garden eastward in Eden, and there he put the man whom he had formed. And out of the ground the Lord God made every tree grow that is pleasant to the sight and good for food. The tree of life was also in the midst of the garden, and the tree of the knowledge of good and evil."*

Then looking back to the first account of creation in Genesis chapter 1, in verse 29, after having created mankind, male and female, are these words,

> *"And God said, See, I have given you every herb that yields seed which is on the face of the earth, and every tree whose fruit yields seed; to you it shall be for food."*

We have already acknowledged that the food God provides sustains more than our bodies but is also food for the soul and spirit. But, for the time being, let's examine the herbs and fruits given to physically sustain us.

From these two verses, we learn a couple of things. First, while these verses do not expressly eliminate meat from the diet of those living in garden, it does strongly suggest that man was created to be a vegetarian. This would go along with Eden being a sanctuary of peace and free of violence, not unlike heaven where *"the wolf and the lamb shall feed together, and the lion shall eat straw like the ox"* (Isa. 65:25). Secondly, God determined that man would need a variety of herbs and fruit to keep him healthy; he would need a balanced diet. *(See chapter 10 for a further discussion of the role of predators in the animal world)*

Just as an aside, the first mention of man ingesting meat in the Bible came after the great flood in Genesis 9:1–3. After the ark came to rest on dry ground, the Lord God made a covenant with Noah which include these words,

> *"Be fruitful and multiply, and fill the earth. And the fear of you and the dread of you shall be on every beast of the earth, on every bird of the air, on all that move on the earth, and on every fish of the sea. They are given into your hands.* Everything that moves shall be food for you. *I have given you all things, even as* (or along with) *the green herbs."*

However, the argument can be made that man also ate meat from the time he was expelled from Eden. For Adam's son, Abel, was a keeper of sheep (Gen. 4:2) which implies that their diet would have included mutton.

All this aside, we repeat, our interest lies in the diet God established for the fullness of life in Eden, that which sustains and enhances quality of life. With one exception, which we will deal with later, there is nothing in Genesis to identify any of the herbs or fruit growing in the garden except to say that many of the fruits were those which had seeds within them. This seems to be important as seeds are the means by which life is perpetuated. The Hebrew word translated as seed is the same in the verses relating to plants as was used when speaking of the descendants of Adam and Eve. It speaks to the means God designed for the assurance that the life and spirit He created could be continued. But it also speaks to the Seed of the woman who is Christ, and the need that we gain our sustenance from Him.

However, none of this really gives us a clue as to the specific nutrients the Lord God determined was absolutely necessary for the health and life of those living in Eden. Yet as we consider who we really are—creatures made in the image of God who is spirit—people whose very life began with the breath of God, that is, His Spirit, a people who were not a people until the Holy Spirit had come upon them; and if we remember the words of Jesus that *"man does not live by bread alone, but by every word that proceeds from the mouth of God"* (Luke 4:4; Deut. 8:3), our consideration of the menu changes. For if as De Chardin has written, "We are spiritual beings having a physical experience," we should look to the Spirit to find the nutrients to sustain our spirits. This then leads to Galatians 5:22.

> *"The fruit of the Spirit is love, joy, peace, patience (longsuffering), kindness, goodness, faithfulness, gentleness, and self-control."*

We readily acknowledge that the New Testament Epistles were written in a post-resurrection world, and Galatians 5 deals specifically with the benefits, or fruit, of living a Spirit-filled life. At the same time, we have to believe life in the garden of Eden, the pre-fall life, was the perfection of Spirit-filled living. If God has chosen to grace Spirit-filled people of our day with these traits, "love, joy, peace, etc.," it stands to reason these would have been powerfully present in our first parents. And if these were to be a part of human character then the means of their nurture would also have been present.

As we have already seen, the two trees identified as being most important in Eden, the tree of life and the tree of the knowledge of good and evil were not specific to the nurture of man's body but also of his soul. So too do these so-called fruits of the Spirit. For while God is concerned about our person, He is more concerned for our souls and our spirits. Thus, following the example of the first two trees mentioned in Genesis, we will use the metaphors "trees" and "fruits" to define the source of each while acknowledging the true source to be the Spirit of God.

For sure, Adam and Eve would have needed ample food and a balanced diet to sustain them physically; and we have been told that this came from fruits, seeds, herbs, etc. But the food now being discussed did not come from the flora around them; it came from their relationship with God. The fruit of the Spirit being considered are those things implied when Jesus said, "*We do not live by bread alone, but by every word that proceeds from the mouth of God.*" As everything proceeding from the mouth of God emits the Spirit of God which feeds all that is life, body, mind, and spirit.

So as our original premise states, we have within us a homesickness for Eden—for life as God intended it to be. Let us further examine the fruits of the Spirit, that is, the nurturing power of God. Even today, while, as much as our hearts and souls desire it, we can't physically return to Eden; we can still draw our sustenance from the "trees" God planted in the garden. Those producing fruits called love, joy, peace, patience, kindness, goodness, faithfulness, gentleness, and self-control as well as hope for renewed access to the tree of life as promised by the life and work of Jesus Christ our Lord and Redeemer.

Perhaps it will help to form an image in our minds of a garden; this is not to say the garden of Eden looked exactly like this. We don't really know, but it could have. Let's envision the tree of life in the middle of the garden. It is huge and lush and beautiful and ever-bearing with tasty fruit. Its roots extend out beyond its branches filling the whole garden, except for that one section where the tree with that forbidden fruit is planted. But surrounding the tree of life are numerous trees of various species, each bearing fruit of their own. The roots of these trees intertwine with those of the tree of life and draw sustenance from it while returning energy to it. Just as our bodies absorb a variety of vitamins and minerals, each serving specific cells and organs within the body, each of these "trees'" benefit us in different ways while contributing to the health of the whole body. They are all different, possessing their own character, yet they exist collectively as a single entity; each is important in its own right but even more so when combined with the others. Each tree's fruit is unique in size and shape; each has its own taste and provides different types and quantities of nutrients, but each contributes to the health of the consumer; each is equally important to his balanced diet.

Let's consider each of the nine trees known by their fruits and revealed to us as the fruit of the Spirit. Trees, like animals and other plants, exist in families. Certain trees share genetic makeup with those in their grouping, what we are inclined to call their common DNA. Indeed, among the fruit of the Spirit, we find some looking very much like others; and these we will deal with collectively. Of all the trees surrounding the tree of life, the one most like it would have to be the tree of love. So what do we know about this tree?

The Tree of Love—God is love! With this brief statement, we have elevated this tree to a plane above all others of the nine. In fact, it would be easy to assume that the other trees would not exist apart from love. This is affirmed in the statement about love Saint Paul made in 1 Corinthians 13. This is the passage of scripture often read at weddings. Perhaps it should be read more often, especially at funerals when we are most reminded of the value of those we love.

> *Love suffers long and is kind; love does not envy, love does not parade itself, is not puffed up; does not behave rudely, does not seek its own, is not provoked, thinks no evil; does not rejoice in iniquity, but rejoices in the truth; bears all things, believes all things, endures all things. Love never fails... And now abide faith, hope, love, these three; but the greatest of these is love.* (1 Cor. 13:4–8a;13)

We encourage the reader to meditate on this passage of scripture, digging into it to hear the voice of God speaking this truth; that love cannot exist singularly. Love is the only entity we hold onto by letting loose of it; it is never ours until we give it away. Love dwells in the heart and thrives as we connect our hearts with the those of others. Love overcomes, overachieves, overreaches, and ever-endures.

There are a few places where love cannot exist; in our egos, in selfishness, in hatred, in prejudice, with injustice, even in sin. The very definition of sin, "that which separates us from God," creates a divide; a chasm between us and the One who is love. And even as love cannot reside in these, it is because of the indomitable capacity of God's love that He sent Jesus as our healer and redeemer. It is love who restores our souls.

> *"God so loved the world that he sent his only begotten Son, that whoever believes in Him should not perish, but have everlasting life"* (John 3:16).

This oft-quoted statement affirms our earlier testimony that the tree of love is forever connected to and a close relative of the tree of life. They are as two trunks off of the same root. Equally important to this passage is its continuation, verse 17, *"For God did not send His Son into the world to condemn the world, but that the world through Him might be saved."*

Here again, we find evidence that even as God removed man from the garden He had prepared for him, He did not remove himself from mankind. In fact, the Apostle John tells us that it is precisely by the acts of God's love that we see and know Him.

> *No one has seen God at any time. If we love one another, God abides in us, and His love has been perfected in us. By this we know that we abide in Him and He in us, because He has given us His Spirit. And we have seen and testify that the Father has sent the Son as Savior of the world. Whoever confesses that Jesus is the Son of God, God abides in Him and he in God. And we have known and believed the love that God has for us. God is love,*

> *and he who abides in love abides in God, and God in him.* (1 John 4:12–16)

Through the power of the Spirit of God in us, we are given the capacity to love. That is, we are given the opportunity to eat of the tree of love and to be nourished by it. And having been nourished through love we can do none other than to love others. And by loving others as Christ loves us, we give them the opportunity to see God. Jesus said, "*A new commandment I give to you, that you love one another; as I have loved you, that you also love one another.*"

As the Lord God prepared the garden as a place for his special creation to dwell and determined all that it would require for this man-child of His to flourish and grow, first among the fruits He provided for him had to be that from the tree of love. He would need to love God; he would need to love others; he would even need to love himself, and since the nature of love requires that he constantly discharge love, this love would require replenishment. To remain healthy, man would need to eat perpetually of the tree of love, that which only God himself can provide.

The passage from John 3:16 gives adequate testimony that life and love are powerfully sustained when joined at the hip, so to say. A person who does not, or cannot, love feels deprived of life, and likewise, a person whose love is constantly rejected can come to believe that life is not worth living. Is love necessary for the body to continue to function as in breathing and possessing a beating heart? Perhaps not. But then if that was all there was, few would call that living. There is a mechanical part of human life which can, if necessary, be artificially sustained by modern medical technique and equipment. But even the medical specialists understand that this isn't really life unless the brain is also functioning. And nothing sustains our brain functions more than love. Nothing strengthens a dying person's will to live more than the bonds they have formed with others through mutual love.

We experience such love; we have learned to live in it through the example of Jesus Christ whose total existence is that of love for

His Father in heaven and love for all men. Perhaps this is summed up in yet another passage of scripture relating to our nurture.

> *I am the true vine, and My Father is the vine dresser. Every branch in Me that does not bear fruit, He takes away, and every branch that bears fruit, He prunes, that it may bear more fruit... I am the vine, you are the branches. He who abides* (lives) *in Me, and I in Him, bears much fruit; for without Me you can do nothing.* (John 15:1–2, 5)

Again, this is using the analogy of fruit, of food for the body, to make a point about the spiritual connection between God and man through the person of His Son, Jesus Christ our Lord. It speaks to the health of this relationship in terms of removing that which is dead and pruning, or cleansing, that which has life in it to give it a stronger and greater life. And the fuel for this relationship is love.

We stated earlier that the garden in all its perfection was prepared specifically as the dwelling place for man. But it also was designed to be the place where God would interact with His created. It was where the Lord walked with him and talked with him and loved him immensely. And it is eternal.

We have maintained from the beginning of this book that the world, specifically Eden, was created as the place where man would dwell. But just as important, is the fact that God created man to be His own companion, to love Him, worship and adore Him. We are made in His image, in the image of He who is love; therefore, the love gene is within us—and it must be fed.

> *"Lord, You have been our dwelling place in all generations. Before the mountains were brought forth, or ever You had formed the earth and the world, from everlasting to everlasting, You are God"* (Ps. 90:1–2).

The Lord is forever; and as He is, so is the tree of love.

> *"The Lord planted a garden eastward in Eden, and there He put the man He had formed. And out of the ground He made every tree grow that is pleasant to the sight and good for food."*

In the very middle of His garden, He planted the tree of life, and from what we have learned of the mind of God, it is most probable that right up close to it He would have established the tree of love.

And God said, "It is very good!"

6

Joyful Peace

Keeping in mind our premise that the trees which the Lord God "planted" in the garden of Eden were necessary for quality of life, not just basic existence, in this chapter, we will examine two additional "trees" identified by their fruit as revealed in Galatians 5. As has been stated, this fruit was then, and still is, necessary for life as the Lord God designed it. We may consider them like a second course in our dining as their benefit is best realized after having our palates titillated by a healthy main course of love—for the benefits of the fruit of the trees of joy and peace are conditional upon a favorable attitude, and thus may be perceived as parasitical to love. Love being the necessary nutrient for a positive attitude and pleasing demeanor.

The Tree of Joy

> *Great is the Lord, and greatly to be praised in the city of our God, in His holy mountain. Beautiful in elevation, the joy of the whole earth, is Mount Zion on the sides of the north, the city of the great King. God is in her palaces; He is known as her refuge… As we have heard, so we have seen in*

> *the city of the Lord of hosts, in the city of our God: God will establish it forever. We have thought, O God, on your loving kindness, in the midst of Your temple. According to Your name, O God, so is Your praise to the ends of the earth.* (Ps. 48:1–3; 8–10a)

The joy of the whole earth resides in the presence of the Lord our God. Thus, declares the psalmist as he looks upon the place God had prepared for him. Such is the joy that comes upon us when we recognize and acknowledge that we are in His holy presence. Such is our elation when we know in our hearts we are precisely where God wants us to be.

Before we can properly discuss the necessity of a healthy diet of joy in our lives, we need to be sure we understand the difference between joy and happiness. Happiness is an emotion; it is the outgrowth of external stimuli. We can be made happy by being in the presence of a favorite person, by receiving a gift, by hearing a kind word, by achieving a goal, etc. But this can be, and often is, fleeting. Our happiness begins to fade as soon as the person or event departs. Then we begin searching for something else to make us happy. A happy person is not necessarily a joyful person. Many a clown has masked his inner sorrow by putting on a happy face and trying to make folks laugh, and many hurting people seek out artificial means of lifting their spirits in a misguided attempt at finding happiness. Laughter, as an outburst of elation, is closely associated with crying stemming from sadness, and their tears are often intermingled.

Joy, on the other hand, is a state of mind. It is an attitude which can exist even within difficult times. It is not dependent upon external stimulus but on internal contentment. It is an attitude gained by understanding who we are in the eyes of God and learning to rejoice in the knowledge that He has us in the palm of His hand. Joyful people are usually known as happy people; after all, happiness is a logical outgrowth of joy. But, again, while joy breeds happiness, happiness in itself is no indicator of joy.

So how do we know we are truly joyful folks? Not surprisingly, the answer is found in holy scripture, particularly in the Psalms. Consider the following as examples:

> *"I will praise the Lord according to His righteousness and will sing praise in the name of the Lord Most High."*

Being confronted by the righteousness of God should draw exultant praise from our lips. Read Psalm 50. It is short and is a song of praise; six verses of instruction on how to praise the Lord. It begins with the words, *"Praise the Lord,"* and ends with, *"Let everything that has breath praise the Lord."*

Praising the Lord not only is the normal reaction to the recognition of His good work in our lives, but it is as fertilizer feeding and strengthening the attitude of joy within us. Joy in itself can be self-perpetuating so long as we don't allow the enemy of our souls steal our joy. That is, joy emits praise to God and such praise feeds joy.

In Paul's letter to the church at Philippi, at the end of chapter 3, verse 20 he speaks *of,*

> *Our citizenship which is in heaven, from which we also eagerly wait for the Savior, the Lord Jesus Christ who will transform our lowly body that it may be conformed to His glorious body, according to the working by which He is able even to subdue all things to Himself.*

And then in Philippians 4:4–7 is this testimony to the presence of joy in the hearts of believers.

> *Rejoice in the Lord always, Again I say, "Rejoice!" Let your gentleness be known to all men. The Lord is at hand. Be anxious for nothing, but in everything by prayer and supplication, with thanks-*

> *giving, let your requests be made known to God, and the peace of God which passes all understanding, will guard your hearts and minds through Jesus Christ.*

Paul has identified certain conditions of our souls which are indicative of a joyful heart. Gentleness, lack of anxiety, being steadfast in prayer, and hearts of thanksgiving are all manifested within the realization that our peace rests in God. As has been stated, joy is a state of mind, but it originates in the heart, in the person who has a heart for God.

> *Sing praise to the Lord, you saints of His, and give thanks at the remembrance of His holy name. For His anger is but for a moment, His favor is for life; weeping may endure for a night, but joy comes in the morning.* (Ps. 30:4–5)

Such assurance should be sufficient to gladden our hearts and instill joy in our souls, but there is more.

Sometimes our joy circulates within us—healing, restoring, feeding, and nurturing us, even as everything around us may be in turmoil. At other times, joy cannot be contained and must come out; it erupts from us as joyful praise, as singing and rejoicing, even spontaneous exultation and dancing. Not surprisingly, we find this in the Bible wherever God's great work is acknowledged and celebrated, and there is no place this occurs more than in the book of Psalms. Following are just a few examples from these Hebrew songs of praise:

> Psalm 31:6 speaks to the mercy of God. *"I will be glad and rejoice in Your mercy, for You have considered my trouble; You have known my soul in adversities and have not shut me up into the hands of my enemies."*

Psalm 33:20 gives praise to God for His faithfulness.

> *"Our soul waits for the Lord; He is our help and our shield. For our heart shall rejoice in Him, because we have trusted in His holy name. Let your mercy, O Lord be upon us, just as we hope in You."*

Psalm 21:1 offers praise for the Lord's saving grace. *"The king shall have joy in Your strength, O Lord, and in Your salvation how greatly shall he rejoice!"*

And finally, Psalm 28:6–7 gives praise for answered prayer. *"Blessed be the Lord, because He has heard the voice of my supplications! The Lord is my strength and my shield; my heart trusted Him, and I am helped; therefore, my heart greatly rejoices, and with my song I will praise Him."*

These and numerous other examples found in Scripture testify that joy should be basic within the people of God; it is holy and pure, not restrained by our circumstances but rising above them. Joy is possible and expected when we keep our focus on the character of Christ and strive to be like Him.

> *"The Spirit himself bears witness with our spirit that we are children of God, and if children, then heirs—heirs of God and joint heirs with Christ, if indeed we suffer with him, that we may also be glorified together"* (Rom. 8:16).

The testimony of scripture is that joy is a necessary component to a healthy life and living in the kingdom of God. As such, it is reasonable that our Creator would have provided this necessary spiritual food to instill, preserve, and nurture joy within us. Is it possible that the fruit of one of the trees God provided for Adam and Eve encouraged and nurtured their joy? The testimony of the Spirit in Galatians 5 suggests it to be so as joy is a product of the Holy Spirit within us.

Already, as we defined our vision of a tree whose fruit is joy, we found the aura of peace as an apt component and companion for joy. Therefore, it seems right to us that God the Creator would have planted within His garden, and very close to the tree of joy, another tree to feed our spirits.

A tree of peace

With the mention of peace, most likely the first thing that comes to mind is the absence of conflict; the cessation of war or the restoration of a relationship. But the peace which is a fruit of the Spirit, and thus, the basis for a supposition that among the many trees God planted in the garden of Eden is one which nurtures a satisfied life, a different peace all together. After all, Eden, as God designed it, would have been free from the negative forces which destroy our peace.

Peace, from a biblical stand point has to do with the state of mind of the individual; it speaks to his tranquility and general well-being. And it always originates with God. So, like joy, peace is much about attitude. It can exist within us even while we are dealing with external turmoil, and it can be absent within while the world around us is at rest and wonderful. Just an observation, it appears that few people in our world today are enjoying peace. Anxiety, anger, hatred, prejudice, selfishness, and the like eat away at our souls and destroy any possibility for peace to reside within us. We have replaced congeniality with contention and made it an art form to the detriment of our peace of mind and calmness of spirit.

Due to this absence of peace, people often seek artificial means of finding it. They turn to mind-numbing chemicals or distractive activities in search of peace. Some try to retreat from reality or give themselves over to unhealthy and often sinful relationships in hopes that they will find peace in someone else. But no one can be our peace other than the Lord who is God.

While we can find many uses of the word peace in the Bible which relates to the absence of conflict, etc., the primary meaning of peace in the Old Testament is completeness or soundness in the well-being of a person. It had to do with his relationship with the

Lord God and was dependent upon being able to follow the Law. Psalm 119:165 says,

> *"Great peace have those who love Your law, and nothing causes them to stumble."*

And in the same psalm, verse 97 we find, *"Oh how I love Your law! It is my meditation all the day."*

In the New Testament, this inner peace rests in Jesus, the self-proclaimed fulfiller of the law. The believer is able to enter into this peace as he surrenders to Christ and puts his trust in him. Testimony of this trait of Christ began even before He was born as the Messianic prophecy of Isaiah 9 states, beginning at verse 7,

> *For unto us a Child is born, unto us a Savior is given; and the government shall be upon His shoulder. And His name shall be called Wonderful, Counselor, Mighty God, Everlasting Father, Prince of Peace. Of the increase of His government and peace there will be no end.*

The Hebrew word translated as peace in this verse is "shalom." It is a common Hebrew greeting from one person to another and carries all the comfortable meanings we associate with peace, health, wealth, and happiness, etc. Of course, the association of Jesus with such peace continued in Luke 2 as he wrote of the circumstances of Christ's birth including this statement from verses thirteen and fourteen,

> *"And suddenly there was with the angel a multitude of the heavenly hosts praising God and saying: Glory to God in the highest, and on earth peace, goodwill toward men."*

The language used in such verses helped the early Hebrews gain an understanding that the coming Messiah's primary purpose was to free them from external pressures. To them He would be that mighty warrior, the everlasting king, who would vanquish the enemy and free them from all foreign rule. Such freedom, in their minds, would then lead to a peace framed within health, wealth, happiness, etc.

But as we move into the New Testament, it doesn't take long for the scholars and rulers of the day to dismiss Jesus as the Messiah because he didn't fit the mold that they had constructed for Him in their minds. Among the earliest words of Jesus recorded in the gospels concerning peace are these disturbing words,

> *"Do not think that I came to bring peace upon the earth. I did not come to bring peace, but a sword"* (Matt. 10:34).

Strange words indeed, for a man who was proclaimed to be the Prince of Peace. But as we continue with Jesus in this thought in verse 38 we hear,

> *"He who does not take up his cross and follow Me is not worthy of Me. He who finds his life will lose it, and he who loses his life for My sake will find it."*

Again, there is not much here to promote a sense of peace, but as we read on and consider all we know about the Gospel of Jesus Christ, we learn just how radical is Jesus's message. Here, Jesus was speaking a truth; a prophetic message to those who were following him that their journey was not going to be easy. In fact, it could result in death, physical death. But ultimately, those who remained steadfast in their allegiance to Him would gain eternal life.

There would be other times when Jesus would address the peace which only He can provide. For example, in John 14, while sitting at the table in the upper room in Jerusalem; having shared the Passover meal with His disciples and soon after having identified Judas as one who would betray Him, Jesus spoke of the *one* He would send to be with them after He departed to heaven, verse 15,

> *"If you love Me, keep my commandments. And I will pray the Father, and He will give you another Helper, that He may abide with you forever—the Spirit of truth..."*

and looking on to verse 25,

> *These things I have spoken to you while being present with you. But the Helper; the Holy Spirit, whom the Father will send in My name, He will teach you all things, and bring to your remembrance all things that I have said to you. Peace, I leave with you, My peace I give to you. Let not your heart be troubled, neither let it be afraid.*

There is a totally different tone stemming from a totally different context in these verses compared to that of Matthew 10. In Matthew, Jesus was speaking of the realities of the world; while in John, He was preparing his disciples for life with the Holy Spirit. These are exact opposite situations. And it is life under the authority of the Spirit of God which is the subject of our text, and the purpose of the tree of peace which feeds our souls and calms our spirits, even when from the world's viewpoint, it doesn't make much sense.

It can only make sense when we trust the Lord and are steadfast in our faith in Him. It makes sense only when we keep our focus on Him in times of trouble and not on the trouble itself. The strong men of God in the scriptures understood this; those whom we hold up as heroes of the faith were those who were able to maintain their focus in the face of ungodly pressures, or those who were able to re-focus on the Lord having once let down their guard and experienced the consequence of their failures.

While under siege by his enemies, King David could write a song of praise, Psalm 138 pledging to *"Praise You with my whole heart,"* and in verse 7 he proclaims,

> *"Though I walk in the midst of trouble, You will revive me; You will stretch out Your hand against the wrath of my enemies, and Your right hand will save me."*

This rather parallels the favorite Psalm of many, Psalm 23 and verse 7 with its verse,

> *"Yea, though I walk through the valley of the shadow of death, I will fear no evil; for You are with me."*

There is a quote from an unknown source that says, "Even in the midst of your worst circumstances you can find peace—because God's got you." This, perhaps, is a restating of the verse previously quoted from Philippians 4:4–7 which includes the phrase, *"The peace of God which passes all understanding, will guard your hearts and minds through Jesus Christ."*

Perhaps this sums up the problem with peace in our lives as much as any. True peace, God's peace, that which comes from Him when we need it most doesn't make sense to those wrapped in worldly constraints; it truly surpasses human understanding. But we don't have to understand it. We just need to live by faith and rejoice in the peace it brings. Romans 5:1–5 is an important summarizing passage to this subject.

> *Therefore, having been justified by faith, we have peace with God through our Lord Jesus Christ, through whom we also have access by faith into this grace in which we stand, and rejoice in hope of the glory of God. And not only that, but we also glory in tribulations, knowing that tribulation produces*

> *perseverance, and perseverance, character; and character, hope. Now hope does not disappoint, because the love of God has been poured out in our hearts by the Holy Spirit who was given to us.*

This same Holy Spirit who bears fruit in us as testified in Galatians 5 and includes the fruits of joy and peace is the Spirit of God who worked with God the Father at creation to plant the trees in the garden of Eden; trees which were designed to fill the needs of the inhabitants of the garden. The fruit of these trees provided the necessities for mankind to assure that we would have everything we would need to maintain healthy bodies, souls, and spirits. After all, we were designed to live forever.

We should not be surprised to find such trees in the grove surrounding the tree of life, and we should not be mystified by the fact that the Holy Spirit continues to provide these same nutrients to us today; nutrients needed to maintain healthy souls for the kingdom of God and to sustain those who abide in the promise of eternal life through their faith in Jesus Christ.

7

GOOD ANYTIME

Sometimes we eat for pleasure or to be sociable more than because of hunger. Hors d' oeuvres, for example, are tasty morsels usually served as appetizers during a social time before the main meal is served. But often these continued to be picked at even after the meal has been completed. In other words, they are good anytime. Typically, these are more than a sampling of off-the-shelf snacks such as mints or nuts, but fancy foods which have required considerable preparation time and energy. Even as these foods by themselves are not intended to constitute a meal, neither would a polite guest ignore them but might even sample each of them.

Such are the remaining fruits of the Spirit (Galatians 5) which invite us to consider those elements of our lives deemed necessary for healthy and fulfilled living. There are several of them perhaps causing us to equate them to a church dinner; what some call a "carry-in" or "pot-luck" where various members bring in the dish of their choice which are then joined with the others and shared among all in attendance. The consumer approaches the table with the intent of being selective focusing on those dishes which he hopes will satisfy his particular taste. But he also is aware of the love and effort put into each dish and does not want to slight anyone; therefore, he tries to sample a bit of each. If he has been unable to accomplish this the first time through, and if he is able to handle a second trip past the tables, he might then select those dishes he missed the first time.

However, we look at it; the remaining fruits of the Spirit are just as important as those we have already highlighted. *Love, joy,* and *peace* must be included in our spiritual diets. For, as Paul summed up his original list in Galatians 5, he concluded, *"Against such there is no law"* (Gal. 5:23b). In other words, partaking of the fruit given by the Spirit can only bring good. If they were harmful to yourself or to others, there would be a law against it.

So let us continue. As in this chapter, we take a look at the remaining six "foods" provided for us as we walk in the Spirit beginning with patience or as it is also called, long-suffering.

The Fruit of Patience

It is a rare person who does not deal with impatience. It is a disease of our culture and a soft target for our enemy, Satan. Our culture encourages us to grab all we can and do it now. Satan tells us we are entitled to it, and if we wait, we might miss out on it. Neither is true. God wants us to learn patience for its foundation is trust in Him. And this is where He wants us to be in a position of submission and obedience such that we not rely on our own faulty senses but on His perfect will.

> *"Those who wait upon the Lord shall renew their strength; they shall mount up with wings like eagles, they shall run and not be weary, they shall walk and not be faint"* (Isa. 40:31).

What is there about patience which elevates it to this list of the fruit of the Spirit? We could go back to the last chapter where we spoke about the fruit of peace and were reminded of Romans 5:1–5 which says,

> *Therefore, having been justified by faith, we have peace with God through our Lord Jesus Christ,*

> *through whom we also have access by faith into this grace in which we stand, and rejoice in hope of the glory of God. And not only that, but we also glory in tribulations, knowing that tribulation produces perseverance, and perseverance, character; and character, hope. Now hope does not disappoint, because the love of God has been poured out in our hearts by the Holy Spirit who was given to us.*

Perseverance and patience in most contexts are synonymous. At the very least, perseverance is patience under stress. If we insert patience for perseverance in this passage, we can see how patience aids in building character and character, hope. Hope itself being an expression of our trust in God. For the definition of biblical hope is not wishful thinking, but confidence in God and His assurance that He loves us and desires us to have all good things—those things necessary for the preservation of our souls.

Waiting is a fact of life and a necessary part of it. A farmer plants the seed and then waits for it to produce a plant and then the fruit which he will harvest. The homemaker prepares the dough and waits for it to rise before placing it in the oven. The vintner harvests the grapes and squeezes out the juice but still has to wait before it becomes wine. And some wines take years to come to peak maturity. The new mother senses the movement in her womb then waits month before she can hold the child in her arms and nurse him; and the Bible is replete with stories of those who awaited the promises of God.

Consider Luke 2:25 which speaks of Simeon, an old and very devout man, who was in the temple when, forty days after Jesus's birth, His parents brought Him along for Mary's required purification rites and sacrifices. Simeon had believed upon the promise he had received from the Lord that, *"He would not taste death until he had seen the Lord Christ."* Then upon seeing the infant Jesus, he took him in His arms and spoke what the Church has labeled the Nunc Dimittis, the Song of Simeon, which begins with the phrase, *"Lord, now you are letting Your servant depart in peace, according to Your word;*

for my eyes have seen Your salvation which you have prepared before the face of your people."

It is evident that, in the grand plan of God, waiting is a necessary process for the gathering of good things. Perhaps it is because the wait adds to the appreciation of the gift; perhaps it is to help us understand the process by which things mature. But mostly, we believe, it instills in us a great appreciation for the continuing work of God, that creation wasn't a one day or one-week venture in which He exhausted all His creative juices and then just sat back and watched us mess it up. Instead, creation and the life the Lord built into it is ongoing; it is constantly being renewed and refreshed. It is, within itself, a reminder that we aren't finished yet. God is still perfecting us preparing us for the eternal life He desires for us.

And this is perhaps the greatest lesson we can learn about patience; the reminder of how patient our Lord God is with us. From 1 Thessalonians 1:3–5, Saint Paul commends this church for their faithfulness and patience.

> *We give thanks to God always for you all, making mention of you in our prayers, remembering without ceasing your work of faith, labor of love, and patience of hope in our Lord Jesus Christ in the sight of God the Father, knowing, beloved brethren, your election by God. For our gospel did not come to you in word only, but also in power, and in the Holy Spirit.*

Both secular and biblical history have shown that the promises of God often take years, even centuries, to come to fruition. Why isn't always easily discerned. In Hebrews 11, we find a litany of great men and women of history who by faith believed the promises of God; men like Noah and Abraham, his wife Sarah and their son Isaac, then Moses, David, Samuel, et al, who all believed in the promise of God yet did not live to see that day come. Today, we live in the promise of Christ's return. Some eagerly await it believing it is very near; others hear this promise and tremble in dread while still others dismiss it all together. But the scriptures are very plain in reporting the Lord's promise to return with only this caveat, He will come on a day and at an hour we will not know in advance, and He will come without warning, "as a thief in the night."

We have already waited nearly two thousand years for this promise, yet it is no less assured and no less anticipated. The Lord's promise is always sure, and His word is always true. From the beginning, God the Father wanted us to understand the need for patience, and he wants us to maintain our faith and trust in Him as we wait patiently upon the Lord.

The fruits of *kindness* and *goodness* are closely related, like two variations of the same species. It can be argued that they are one and the same as kindness is an outgrowth of the goodness within us. Goodness, in the biblical sense, is more than good actions; it is a matter of the heart. It emits from the God who is in us and speaks to our character. Kindness, then, is more a description of our actions toward others; it is goodness demonstrated.

Kindness requires a sensitivity to the needs of others coupled with a love for mankind. It is often manifest as compassion and mercy—traits which are modeled for us by our Lord Jesus Christ. Goodness, on the other hand, rests in our character and speaks to the presence of the Spirit within us.

One mistake people often make when labeling a person or group as Christian is they make this determination based on their judgment that "they are good people." But being good does not make one Christian; likewise, many non-Christians do good things. Being Christian is believing that Jesus Christ is Lord. He is our Savior. And the level of kindness and goodness we are discussing here is that existing as fruits of the Spirit. That is, they are manifest in us because the Holy Spirit is within us. And if the Holy Spirit is within us, then the kindness and goodness evident in us is an outpouring of the love and mercy of Christ in us.

Like other of the fruits of the Spirit, kindness and goodness are not traits we control but are given over to the work of the Spirit. In this sense, we are merely vessels, the tools, which God uses to do His work in the world. It is possible for misguided people, and those under the influence of the enemy to misuse these gifts. Even believers, with all good intentions, can embark on a mission speared on by their own will and strength and apart from the will of God, only to find it come to no good end. It is always a devastating event when our best efforts to help others results in negative circumstances. Surely, it is the Lord's desire that good things come to good people, but our involvement need be dependent upon the will of God and in His timing.

The goodness defined as a fruit of the Spirit in Galatians 5 is that characterized by righteousness, holiness, love, mercy, and the like—all evidences of Christ in us. He is the model and incentive for us as we continue to live and work in His kingdom. In Matthew 6, the passage is urging us not to worry about things we can't control. Jesus instructs us, *"Seek first the kingdom of God and His righteousness, and all these things shall be added to you."* This is a statement of truth for all believers and encouragement for us to meditate on His word so as to know and be strengthened in His abiding presence.

Next in the list of fruits of the Spirit is *Faithfulness* also called steadfastness, a word which sounds much like it's meaning, standing fast or firm in commitment. It is about dependability and loyalty, being true to our word and our calling. In our context, it is holding firm in our commitment to the Lord and to the life to which He has called us.

For our purposes, we are separating *faithfulness* as a fruit of the Spirit from *faith* as a gift of the Spirit as listed in 1 Corinthians 12:9. While grammatically connected, they speak to quite different and unique characteristics of a person and his relationship with Christ and thus are being dealt with separately in this study. Faith is the subject of chapter 9. Herein, we will discuss faithfulness as a positive and desirable characteristic of mankind rising out of his relationship with the Lord—that which flowers within us as we are immersed in the Holy Spirit.

Like other aspects of our life in the Lord, we look to God as our example. Throughout scripture, we are reminded of the faithfulness of God, the One who always keeps His covenants. Lamentations 3:22–23 proclaims,

> *"Through the Lord's mercies we are not consumed, because His compassions fail not. They are new every morning; great is Your faithfulness. The Lord is my portion says my soul, therefore I hope in Him!"*

This thought is echoed and amplified in Psalm 89 which begins,

> *"I will sing of the mercies of the Lord forever; with my mouth will I make known your faithfulness to all generations. For I have said, 'Mercy shall be built up forever; Your faithfulness You shall establish in the very heavens.'"*

And then in verse 8, *"O Lord God of hosts, who is mighty like You, O Lord? Your faithfulness also surrounds You. You rule the raging of the sea; when its waves rise, You shall still them."*

The testimonies of God's faithfulness abound in scripture through the graces of deliverance from temptation, the assurance of our salvation and the forgiveness of sins.

> *"If we confess our sins, He is faithful and just to forgive us our sins and cleanse us from all unrighteousness"* (1 John 1:9).

These are not mere words but are manifest in our own experiences and in the testimony of millions.

However, God never intended that such faithfulness be His alone, but that it be reflected in the hearts and lives of the people. Earlier in speaking of the fruit of the Spirit called patience or persistence we mentioned Hebrews 11 and the list of saints who believed God and patiently awaited His promises. These all stayed steadfast in their belief and confidence in God even as they did not live to see the fulfillment of the promise. Indeed, this passage of scripture, sometimes called the *Faith Hall of Fame,* is acknowledgement of their faithfulness to the promise of God.

Faithfulness is expected of the Christian believer. Sometimes the gathering of God's people is simply called, "the Faithful," as in Psalm 31:23,

> *"Oh, love the Lord, all you His saint! For the Lord preserves the faithful and repays the proud person. Be of good courage, and He shall strengthen your heart, all you who hope in the Lord."*

Any discussion concerning our faithfulness to God has to include the word dependency. We can be faithful to God as we learn to trust Him and be totally dependent upon Him. And we demonstrate our faithfulness as we remain steadfastness in the faith and become people others can trust, that is, we become dependable in ourselves. This we learn to do as we become open and dependent upon the Holy Spirit to lead and direct our lives.

The inclusion of such traits as steadfastness or faithfulness among those listed as the fruit of the Spirit is a good indication that these same traits were to be present in the people God prepared to live in the garden of Eden. Therefore, we surmise that among the herbs and trees God planted to feed Adam and Eve would have been those which would have nurtured these assets.

Finally, we consider the remaining two items listed as fruit of the Spirit—*Gentleness and Self-control.* In these also, we see a strong connection as it often requires a bit of self-control to act with gentleness, especially in confrontational situations, and gentleness often is a sign of one who is in control of his emotions. But both are rare apart from the presence of the Holy Spirit.

Yes, there are those who are naturally easy-going, quiet, respectful; traits often equated with gentleness and who may have no obvious affiliation with the Holy Spirit. And there are those who have learned the science of maintaining control of their emotions apart from any faith experience. Yet there is a dimension to the fruit of the Spirit which separates these from those who are spirit-filled.

Gentleness is similar to meekness in that, from the world's point of view, they are often perceived as weakness. They are associated with those who have no spunk or drive, who are content to sit back and let others lead. Yet Christ, our supreme example of meekness and gentleness, was the exact opposite. He is known for the power in His voice, the authority in His teaching, and the commitment to His calling, even when it meant suffering and eventually submitting to death.

Meekness itself is defined as humility before God and gentleness before men stemming from the realization that God is in control. When a person knows there is a power greater than himself, there is no room for puffing up oneself or making a show of his attempt to be in control of a situation. Instead, the gentle person is more likely to be respected and heard.

Self-control is like it in that it is a matter of the will. The Christian who is governed by God rather than by self is more likely to maintain control in stressful situations and be more reliable in decision making. While gentleness is closely related to personality, self-control is a learned skill, and one that is enhanced by the presence of the Holy Spirit. But both arise from the same source, the authority and example of Christ with the ever-present power of the Holy Spirit. And both become very effective tools when fighting the forces of evil, especially those which otherwise would distort the truth of God in us.

Having made a big assumption, yet one which fits logically within our premise that Eden was made for man and not the other way around, that the fruit of the Spirit as identified by Saint Paul in Galatians 5 is a reflection upon the "foods" the Lord God provided to nurture mankind in Eden, we can begin to understand what God had in mind for man from the beginning. That is, there are certain traits, certain expectations of man for which God provided and nurtured in Eden, and these are the same traits and expectations He made available for men on earth through the power of the Holy Spirit. Even as man fell from grace by his disobedience and was exiled from his primordial home, the Lord still provides opportunity for us to feed from these same fruits.

So far, we have primarily dealt with the fruit bearing trees of Eden, that which best equates to "food" for the body. There remain other trees as mentioned in Genesis 2; those which are pleasing to the eyes. Next, we will explore what these might be and consider their value.

8

EYE CANDY

So far, we have dealt with the fruit of the Spirit as presented in Galatians 5 and have hypothesized that these would also have been present in Eden. That is, since God the Father has sent the Holy Spirit to us at Jesus's request, and if this Spirit inspires such valuable and necessary traits in us, it stands to reason that the Father would also have provided for the development of these same traits in the human inhabitants of Eden, development which would necessitate the availability of nutrients. But we have yet to address the second and equally important part of the description of Eden; we find in Genesis 2:9, *"And out of the ground the Lord God made every tree grow that is pleasant to the sight."*

This is an interesting statement as it assigns a level of necessity to beautiful things, to things that are pleasing to the eye. In fact, if one wanted to be really rigid in his interpretation, he could claim that since this provision precedes that of those being good for food. This "eye candy" is even more important. We are not ready to make that claim but will agree the evidence points to equality of their worth for the growth and health of humankind. Indeed, it is possible that this statement means nothing more than that the nurturing power of God is both good for food and pleasing to the eye. However, as we further explore the Scriptures, we find ample evidence that the Lord

God has built within us a desire, even a need, to be surrounded by His beauty.

Earlier we reminded our readers of the Lord's statement in Deuteronomy 8:3 that,

> *"Man does not live by bread alone, but by every word that proceeds from the mouth of God."*

A statement Jesus quoted as he dismissed the temptations of Satan while in the wilderness. Combine this with the statement from Genesis 2, and we come to understand that while food is necessary for the maintenance of a healthy body, we also need the things that enter us through other of our senses, especially sight and sound. And this is primarily because these things, the sounds we hear and the sights we see, do not enter our stomachs but enter our hearts and our minds. These are not substances which pass through our system and then are eliminated but enter our hearts and become who we are.

Not surprisingly, the Bible speaks a lot about beauty, and mostly, it is in reference to the Lord God, both the Father and the Son. Psalm 27:1,4 is a ready example.

> Verse 1, *"The Lord is my light and my salvation; whom shall I fear? The Lord is the strength of my life; of whom shall I be afraid?"* Verse 4, *"One thing I have desired of the Lord; that I will seek: That I may dwell in the house of the Lord all the days of my life, to behold the beauty of the Lord, and to inquire of his temple."*

This Psalm, like many others, speaks to the desire of its writer to be in the presence of the Lord, interact with Him, and to enjoy His divine beauty. This speaks to the stated premise of this book, that we have within us a strong desire to return to Eden; the place where Adam walked with God, talked with Him, and enjoyed Him as friend and companion.

But God is spirit, and we are flesh and blood. Since the fall of man, we have been separated from God and unable to see His face. We have been unable to see his beauty except as revealed through the prophets, through God's word and deed; that is until Jesus. But even then, the Scriptures reveal a different picture of Jesus. Hear this from Isaiah 53 beginning at verse 2,

> *For He shall grow up before Him as a tender plant, and as a root from dry ground. He has no form or comeliness; and when we see Him there is no beauty that we should desire Him. He is despised and rejected by men, a Man of sorrows and acquainted with grief. And we hid our faces from Him; He was despised and we did not esteem Him.*

This description of the Messiah, the suffering servant, doesn't fit at all with the beautiful Lord described in the Psalms and elsewhere in scripture. It leaves us cold and wondering what this is all about until we read on and discover the character of Christ. Skipping through verses 4 through 6 we learn more.

> *"He has borne our griefs." "He was wounded for our transgressions, bruised for our iniquities." "By His stripes we are healed." "The Lord has laid on Him the iniquity of us all."*

The beauty in Christ is in His character, within his person. It's only as we get to know him that we look beyond his physical appearance and begin to see the Man who is God.

This is exactly the point. Human nature being what it is; we are attracted to the lovely, the popular, and the wealthy. We flock to view the Adonis's of our age and culture; those we idolize and call stars; those we elevate to near godlike status. Yet far too often, we learn that these beautiful people are not so beautiful in character and spirit. Many are downright ugly on the inside. But Jesus is the opposite. God did not want us to flock to Him just to admire His beautiful features. He wants us to know Him and love Him for who He is on the inside. He wants us to join in a relationship with Him which will develop and enhance a desire in us to be like Him.

From the beginning, we are told; we are made in God's image. In the image of them, Father, Son, and Spirit, we are made. And being in His image means having His nature, and being with His nature means that we should represent His beauty. Consider the following:

> *For we are His workmanship, created in Christ Jesus for good works, which God prepared beforehand that we should walk in.* (Eph. 2:10)

> *Therefore do not lose heart. Even though the outward man is perishing, yet the inward man is being renewed day by day.* (2 Cor. 4:16)

> *I will praise You, for I am fearfully and wonderfully made; marvelous are Your works, and that my soul knows very well.* (Ps. 139:14)

These scriptures and others testify to the perfect work accomplished by God, and that His work is beautiful; it is pleasing to the eye. And even as we are stained by the world around us, even as we are marred by disease and death, even as we are scarred by the sin within us, the promise of God is that He is renewing our beauty—our inward beauty—day by day.

Jesus cautioned his disciples to not look at the outward appearance of a man but to look at his deeds and see his heart; just as God does not consider our outward appearance but knows our hearts. In Luke 16:15, he spoke to the Pharisees who derided his teachings telling them,

> *"You are those who justify yourselves before men, but God knows your heart."*

We cannot hide our true selves from the Lord, and we will not escape His judgment.

It is in this vein that we are called to seek the heart of God, to meditate on His word and seek His beauty.

> *Finally, brethren, whatever things are true, whatever things are noble, whatever things are just, whatever things are pure, whatever things are lovely, whatever things are of good report, if there is any virtue and if there is anything praise worthy—meditate on these things.* (Phil. 4:8)

Meditation on the things of the Lord is feasting on Him. As we inwardly digest His word and consider the depths of His wisdom, we are fed spiritually and as our spirits are satiated so will be our bodies and our souls.

The goal of such feasting is to know the heart of God; it is dwelling in the beauty of His holiness.

> *"O worship the Lord in the beauty of holiness! Tremble before Him, all the earth"* (Ps. 96:9). *"And let the beauty of the Lord our God be upon us and establish the work of our hands for us"* (Ps. 90:17).

Among the trees God planted in Eden were those that were pleasing to the sight. Nothing could be more pleasing than to see and to know the Lord our God. Most assuredly among those trees and herbs which the Lord provided were those which nurtured in us the ability and desire to see the beauty of the Lord and of all that He created.

It would be difficult to find a person so hardened of heart and whose mind was so infected by the poison of cynicism that they could not appreciate the beauty of God's created world. Even in its fallen state, even having suffered the ravages of evil and abuse, the world for the most part is a marvelous and beautiful place. Who cannot stand on the rim of the Grand Canyon or look out over a mountain vista and not be in awe of its beauty? Who cannot be amazed by an ever-changing seascape or find beauty in the undulating sand dunes of an otherwise barren desert? Who has not walked a forest trail or trod gently through a blooming meadow and marveled at the unending display? Some even become so taken up by this beauty that they begin to think this has to be God. But it's not God; it is a mere reflection of Him.

The beauty the psalmist, the poet, the lyricist, try to define as being representative of God is beyond words; it is like trying to draw a picture of God and finding that nothing quite measures up. Michelangelo and other great artists may have come close, but how do you put dimension to One who is Spirit? How does one put a frame around One who is infinite and eternal?

As always, we look again to the scriptures where there is really only one word given which comes close to defining the beauty of God. It is "glory." It speaks to the totality of God, His beauty, power, and honor—the total greatness of God. We have given it a name, "glory," yet it eludes us; it is beyond our understanding.

> *"The Lord is high above all nations, His glory above the heavens. Who is like the Lord our God, who dwells on high, who humbles Himself to behold the things that are in the heavens and in the earth?"* (Ps. 113:4–6).

This is the attraction; we strongly desire to live in this glory to be surrounded by it, yet we remain separated from Him for the same reason Adam was separated because of our sinfulness.

> *But now, the righteousness of God apart from the law is revealed, being witnessed by the Law and the Prophets, even the righteousness of God, through faith in Jesus Christ, to all and on all who believe. For there is no difference; all have sinned and fallen short of the glory of God, being justified freely by His grace through the redemption that is in Christ Jesus.* (Rom. 3:21–24)

This glory, this beauty of God is described in the Old Testament as a pillar of cloud and of fire; it is that which shone in the tabernacle and in the temple, and it shone on Moses's face after being in the presence of God such that the people could not look at him requiring that he veil his face until the glory faded.

In the New Testament, this glory is shown mainly in Christ as per the incident on the Mount of Transfiguration where His whole person, clothing and all, were transformed into a glorious array of light. The Apostle John also spoke of this glory in terms of the miracle he did at a wedding in Cana (John 2:11). This, John declares, was a manifesting of His glory resulting in changed hearts in disciples who believed in Him.

John further declares that members of the Church may share in this glory. This is Jesus's prayer as He prepares to go out to Gethsemane to face His betrayers.

> *And now, O Father, glorify Me together with Yourself, with the glory I had with You before the world was. I have manifested Your name to the men whom You have given Me out of the world. They were Yours, You gave them to Me, and they have kept Your word. (John 17:5–6)*

And then in verses 22–23 Jesus further prays,

> *And the glory which You gave Me, I have given them, that they may be one, Just as We are one. I in them, and You in Me; that they may be made perfect in one, and that the world may know that You have sent Me, and have loved them as You have loved Me.*

While this prayer is giving testimony to the lives of the disciples, it also speaks to the process by which Christians are being transformed into the glorious image of God. Believers will not be fully glorified until the end of time when they sit in God's heavenly presence, as described in John's vision of heaven in the Revelation of Jesus Christ, but are being transformed into this glory as they walk with Christ.

In 2 Corinthians 3 Paul reminds us of the veil Moses wore and how Christ has taken away that veil. He has opened the gate for us to enter into God's glory.

> *Unlike Moses, who put a veil over his face so that the children of Israel could not look steadily at the end of what was passing away. But their minds were blinded. For until this day the same veil remains unlifted in the reading of the Old Testament, because the veil is taken away in Christ. But even to this day, when Moses is read, a veil lies on their heart. Nevertheless, when one turns to the Lord the veil is taken away. Now the Lord is Spirit, and where the Spirit of the Lord is, there is liberty. But we all, with unveiled face, beholding as in a mirror the glory of the Lord, are being transformed into the same image from glory to glory, just as by the Spirit of the Lord.* (2 Cor. 3:13–18)

We are not permitted to see the face of God, but we have seen Christ; and in Christ and through Christ, we have witnessed the glory of God. This glory is being developed in the believer as we are being transformed into His likeness, from glory to glory, it says. Thus, when we see people who are deeply in tune with God, we recognize that glory. We are likely to exclaim, "He/She has Christ all over them." This is the indescribable glory of God, indescribable yet palpable, revealed to us as we know Him, love Him, and long to be in His presence forever. This is His overpowering presence in Eden. This is the seed that causes us to be homesick for Eden.

Now, being in the presence of God's glory in Christ Jesus must surely elicit in us a response—a response of praise. For praise is really the only faculty we have to acknowledge God's glory. From beginning to end in the Bible, the people's response to the presence of

God, individually and corporately, has been praise; exultant praise, singing, dancing, chanting, praying, giving glory to God for all His mighty works.

Praise by definition is an act of worship. It acknowledges the greatness of the One being praised. While we may heap praise on those favored in this world, the highest and purest form of praise is that of man toward God. It is the means by which we express our joy to the Lord; praise for who He is and for what He does.

> *Praise the Lord! Praise God in His sanctuary; praise Him in His mighty firmament. Praise Him for His mighty acts; praise Him according to His excellent greatness! Praise Him with the sound of trumpet; praise Him with lute and harp! Praise Him with timbrel and dance; praise Him with stringed instruments and flutes. Praise Him with loud cymbals; praise Him with clashing cymbals! Let everything that has breath praise the Lord. Praise the Lord!* (Ps. 150)

Anyone who, because of the pressures of life, find it difficult to give due praise to the Lord God should recite this Psalm. In fact, a regimen of reading Psalms 147 through 150 will enhance anyone's glorification of God.

The subject for this chapter was developed from the description of Eden as found in Genesis 2: 9 that, *"Out of the ground the Lord God made every tree grow that is pleasant to the sight and good for food."*

This has led us to consider what the Lord wants us to understand about things that are "pleasing to the sight." Our own experiences should be sufficient to teach us the necessity of beautiful things and beautiful people in our lives. They are as soul food; they nourish us in ways the food that goes into our stomach cannot. Where the food we eat gets processed in our bodies, enters our blood stream, and eventually go to our hearts where it is pumped to the organs where it is needed, the things which touch us, the beautiful things of life go immediately to our hearts and feed us, body, soul, and spirit.

But more than anything else, being fed by the "trees" defined as pleasing to the eye reveals the truth that the beauty in the world around us is designed specifically to draw our attention and our desire to the beauty of the Lord. The very nature of God is beauty in that He possesses everything desirable to man—everything that is good and righteous, everything that is true and noble, everything that is worthy. And He has provided that we who are made in His image be beneficiaries of His beauty.

Yet the true value of our appreciation for all things beautiful lies in the fact that they point the way to the glory of God. The more we learn to see and appreciate the beauty around us, not just the majestic splendor of nature, not only the magnificent works of art divinely inspired men and women have produced, but the beauty that is found in the simple and mundane, that encountered in our daily living and that found growing in special relationships; these are our primary and secondary school; these are our university preparing us to stand in the presence of the *eternal glory!*

God, in His infinite wisdom, designed beautiful things to prepare us, to nurture us in preparation for residing in His glory. Originally for eternal life in Eden and now for an eternity in the company of glory everlasting in the arms of God forever. This is why God provided trees in His garden which produced fruit that was good for sight. It was so that we could become that which He first envisioned, reflections of His glory—images of God.

9

The Staple of Faith

In the previous chapter, we spoke of the trees in the garden of Eden which were specific to being pleasing to the eyes, what we called "Eye Candy." And in that chapter, we tried to direct your focus on things deemed to be beautiful because they point us to the nature and glory of God. Within this chapter and elsewhere, we have also mentioned the scripture from Matthew 4:4 where Jesus says, "*Man does not live by bread alone, but by every word that proceeds from the mouth of God.*" Since we have been speaking specifically about those "fruits" and other entities God has supplied in Eden for the nurture of His favored of creation, mankind, we need to learn all we can about this particular statement. As we have for other aspects of human growth and nurture, we begin by looking outside the book of Genesis for clues as to the specific nature and purpose of another element of God's provision for man, one we are calling a "staple" of his life.

Let's begin by setting the stage; the place and circumstance for the statement beginning with the words, "*Man does not live by bread alone.*" In the Gospel of Matthew chapter 3, we learn of the preaching of John the Baptist of how he came into the wilderness of Judea preaching a message of baptism for the remission of sins. John himself was an unusual character, drawing attention even because of his dress, being reminiscent of a prophet of old. Further, he was bringing a message a bit different than that people were used to hearing. And for sure the setting was unusual, as those called to preach, the priests and Levites usually spoke in the temple or in public squares. But even more than this, the people's curiosity was aroused as John spoke as a prophet, and there had not been a prophet in Israel for four hundred years.

From the last Old Testament prophet Malachi, we find in the prophecy looking forward to the coming Messiah with these words, *"Behold I will send you Elijah, the prophet, before the coming day of the Lord. And he will turn the hearts of the fathers to the children, and the hearts of the children to their fathers, lest I come and strike the earth with a curse"* (Mal. 4:5–6).

John certainly looked the model of what people envisioned Elijah to have been, and his message was encouraging, providing an avenue for forgiveness of one's sins. Further John stated to any who would enquire as to if he might be the Messiah that he was not but was, "*The voice of one crying in the wilderness: 'Prepare the way of the Lord; make his paths straight'*" (Matt. 3:3). This being a quote from Isaiah 40, a well-known verse assuring the coming of the Messiah.

So there was much interest in John and perhaps even more consternation among those of the Jewish leadership as they were forced to consider if he was indeed a prophet, or perhaps, just another hermit who had spent too many years roaming in the wilderness.

Then as we pick up the gospel story in Matthew 3:13, we learn that Jesus came from Galilee to John to be baptized. John, realizing in his spirit who Jesus is, did not consider himself worthy to baptize the Messiah. But Jesus insisted that it was right he do so, *"Permit it to be so now, for thus it is fitting for us to fulfill all righteousness"* (verse 15).

This does not suggest that Jesus had to be baptized to atone for sin of His own. He was without sin but that he identified with the believing remnant of Israel who had come to be so baptized and perhaps as a sign that in God's timing, He would take on our sin. In any regard, the baptism of Jesus represented more than spiritual cleansing. For Jesus, it was his ordination, his coronation, if you will, announcing to the world that the Lord had come. Granted, the world did not hear it at that moment, but Jesus did and John did;

and perhaps a few others who saw *"the heavens opened and the Spirit of God descending like a dove and alighting upon Him, and who heard a voice from heaven saying, 'This is My beloved Son, in whom I am well pleased'"* (Matt. 3:16b–17), a declaration demonstrating the cooperation of all three persons of the Godhead, The Father, the Son, and the Holy Spirit.

"Then Jesus was led up by the Spirit into the wilderness to be tempted by the devil" (Matt. 4:1). We pause here to point out a common misconception about the tempting of Jesus. He was *not* led into the wilderness by the devil but by the Holy Spirit. It was God's will that He faced this trial. Likewise, we emphasize that this trial was not due to any displeasure God had with His Son. The Father was not displeased with Him, rather it was a time of preparation.

Jesus would be facing an enemy, a formidable foe. The same enemy who had persuaded God's chosen creature to deny and desert Him. The preparation for any soldier who is likely to stand face-to-face against the enemy is to prepare him for that eventuality and to expose him to battle situations in a controlled manner. God, through the Holy Spirit, led Jesus out into the wilderness where he would suffer physical hardship, where he would be weakened for want of food and battered by the elements, where he might be tempted to listen to anyone who would offer him an easy way out.

We learn from Matthew 4:2 that Jesus had fasted; that is, he had nothing to eat for forty days and forty nights, and He was hungry. It was at this moment Satan came to him and tried to attack at what he supposed would be His weakest point, saying, *"If you are the Son of God, command that these stones become bread."* But Jesus answered and said, "*It is written, 'Man shall not live by bread alone, but by every word that proceeds from the mouth of God.'*"

It may seem that we have gone a long way around the bush to get back to this statement; the foundation for the message we are bringing. But, hopefully, hearing this background and understanding the process by which Jesus was preparing for the work to which God had called him will also instill in us the great truth that all nourishment, that for body, mind, and spirit, comes *from_the mouth of God.* It did then, and it does now.

Let's look closely at this first of the three means by which the devil tempted Jesus. First, he begins by saying, "*If you are the Son of God…* " Remember how the serpent had tempted Adam and Eve by first casting doubt on the truthfulness of God. *"Has God indeed said, 'You shall not eat of every tree of the garden?'"* When Eve responded that God told them not to eat of the tree in the midst of the garden, or they would die. The serpent challenged God's word further, *"You shall not die"* and then, he in essence said, "God just told you that so that he could keep the fruit of this tree to himself. He knows that if you eat of this tree you will be as smart as He is." Casting doubts on God's word and on His motive for speaking worked the first time, so the Satan tried again. He really has nothing new to offer.

But Jesus didn't listen, instead he not only spoke, but he demonstrated the truth of His statement, *"Man does not live by bread alone, but by every word which proceeds from the mouth of God."*

Satan doesn't give up without a fight so he offered a new temptation, and this time he tried to use Jesus's own tactics against Him—by quoting scripture.

> *"Then the devil took Him up into the holy city, set Him on the pinnacle of the temple, and said to Him, 'If You are the Son of God, throw yourself down. For it is written,' "He shall give His angels charge over you, and in their hands they shall bear you up, lest you dash your foot against a stone."*

Jesus said to him, "*It is written again, 'You shall not tempt the Lord your God.'"*

So the devil tried a third time, this time taking Him up on a high mountain where they could see all the kingdoms of the earth. These, the devil offered to Jesus if only He would bow down and worship him. But again, Jesus fended him off by quoting the word of God.

> *"Then Jesus said to him, 'Away with you, Satan! For it is written,' "You shall worship the Lord your God, and Him only you shall serve."*

Three times Satan had thrown temptations at Jesus, offering him the things that he assumed would cause Jesus to falter: food when he is hungry, power to impress and influence others, and gaining authority over peoples and lands—what the Apostle John would call "*the lust of the flesh, the lust of the eyes, and the pride of life*" (1 John 2:16).

It is interesting that, in fending off these temptations, Jesus chose three scriptures found in the book of Deuteronomy, "*Man does not live by bread alone*" (Deut. 8:3). "*You shall not tempt the Lord your God*" (Deut. 6:16). "*You shall worship the Lord your God and only Him shall you serve*" (Deut. 6:13). These verses had all been spoken to a people undergoing their own trial and testing in the wilderness; they were part and parcel to the same great assembly in which the Law, the Ten Commandments, had been given, and these were warnings against doubting the will and power of God. These had been given to impress upon the people the truth that God loved them, and that he had called them out into this period of trial in order to prepare and lead them to the Promised Land. For it is true, we can't truly understand God's grace if we have not first understood our need for deliverance. There are a lot of reasons why God had his people wandering about in the wilderness, chief among them being their own obstinacy and failure to trust Him. Yet, in His timing, God chose to deliver them.

This was the same mission Jesus was sent to accomplish, the deliverance of the people. Not deliverance from political rulers as many supposed to be the purpose of the coming Messiah, but deliverance from the curse placed upon the earth at the time of Adam's expulsion from Eden; and deliverance from the sentence of death which accompanied our sin of pride and disobedience. And this deliverance comes by the way of the Bread of Life.

> "*I am the bread of Life, He who comes to Me shall never hunger, and he who believes in Me shall never thirst,*" Jesus said (John 6:48).

Let's return to Eden, to the garden as God designed it to be the home for this man whom He had made in His image. We have stated over and over that this garden was planted with man in mind. It was to be his forever home. And this garden was complete. It contained every herb, every tree, every seed and fruit necessary to sustain this creature, forever. God had foreseen his need for physical food and for emotional food, (things of beauty) and now we see that He has also provided spiritual food—His very presence. And the recognition and acknowledgement of His presence begins with faith.

In chapter 7 we spoke of faithfulness as one of the *fruits* of the Spirit listed in Galatians 5:22, but faith is identified separately as a *gift* of the Spirit in 1 Corinthians 12:9. Faith is unique among the gifts of the Spirit in that while all the gifts noted are given to individuals within the body of believers to be used for the benefit of all, faith alone is a necessary component of every believer and is vital for his spiritual health. In fact, Saint Paul, in his lead up to identifying the gifts of the Spirit, says this,

> *Now concerning spiritual gifts, brethren, I do not want you to be ignorant: You know that you were Gentiles, carried away to these dumb idols, however you were led. Therefore, I make known to you that no one speaking by the Spirit of God calls Jesus accursed, and no one can say that the Jesus is Lord except by the Holy Spirit.* (1 Cor. 12:1–3)

This speaks not only to the presence and power of the Holy Spirit, but to the gift of faith which is a gift of this same Spirit. Saint Paul rightly affirms that a mark of the true believer is his testimony of Jesus Christ that He is Lord. This, a true believer will never deny.

Life in the garden of Eden was life in the presence of the Holy Spirit; therefore, faith should have been easy in Eden. Everything a man could ever want was provided for him; everything was perfect. He even had God as his personal companion. So what was there to cause man to fall? What could persuade man to question the authority of God?

The answer is *doubt*. Evil inspired doubt! "*Did God really say that if you ate from that tree you would die?*" Satan asked. "*No, you're not going to die. God just wanted to keep that fruit for himself. God knows if you eat from that tree you will be as smart as He is*" (Gen. 3:1,4 paraphrased)?

It's easy for us to see the temptation. Planting the seed of doubt was all it took for Adam's faith to waiver. In chapter 3 we discussed reasons why God would even plant the tree of the knowledge of good and evil. Why would He even allow Adam to be so tempted? And the simplest answer, one we didn't give earlier but do now, is, "To give his faith an opportunity to grow."

Perhaps we are in danger of wearing out our reference to the simple scripture, "*Man does not live by bread alone*" (Deut. 8:3 and Matt. 4:4), but the understanding of this is important. Bread is the staple of life. In Jesus's day, it was the primary means of converting grains into a tasty and portable food. Bread combined with meat supplements and enhances any meal. Even today, bread in some form is available at nearly every meal. Planning for future meals almost always includes bread. With every forecast of coming storms, there is a run on the stores to buy the staples of our pantries. Chief among which is bread. Even among those who normally eat little bread, there seems to be this need to have bread on hand. There is this sense of comfort in the knowledge that having sufficient bread enhances our opportunity for survival.

Well, if bread is the staple of life, then faith is the staple of our character. Consider that Moses stood on the side of the mountain having just explained to the people that they were about to enter the Promised Land, but that he would not be going with them. His time was over and another would lead them. He had just given them the law and other related instructions and then as recorded in Deuteronomy 8 he began to review where they had been.

> *Every commandment which I command you today you must be careful to observe, that you may live and multiply, and go in and possess the land of which the Lord swore to your fathers. And you shall remember that the Lord your God led you all the*

> *way these forty years in the wilderness, to humble you and test you, to know what was in your heart, whether you would keep His commandments or not. So, He humbled you, and allowed you to hunger, and fed you with manna which you did not know nor did your fathers know, that He might make you know that man shall not live by bread alone, but man lives by every word that proceeds from the mouth of the Lord.* (Deut. 8:1–4)

Moses went on to remind these folks of every blessing they had received and cautioned them in several ways to be sure that they kept their focus on the Lord and were steadfast in their faith and obedience to Him. In this way, you shall live and multiply was the strong message of that day.

"Man lives by every word that proceeds from the mouth of the Lord." Our review of creation from Genesis 1 and 2 has emphasized the fact the God spoke into being every element, every rock and tree, every herb and seed, every creature on earth and in heaven. In man, we learned that God further breathed His own breath into him to impart upon him His own Spirit, making him to be in His likeness. Nothing was made that was made which did not originate in the mind of God and emit from the mouth of God.

As Moses would later remind his people, God wants only one thing in return—that we love Him with all our hearts and souls and minds and that we remain obedient to Him, giving Him the honor and glory due His name. It was no different for Adam. In chapter 3, we also stated that the reason God even planted a tree which bore forbidden fruit was a matter of love. If love is to exist, it has to be free. Love has to be free to choose or it's not love. Therefore, if God is to be loved, there has to be an alternative, the option of rejecting God's love. As difficult as this is, the option to reject love sits right beside the option to embrace it.

Moses had to remind the folks in his charge that God had been gracious in their aimless wandering as they sought hundreds and thousands of ways to make it through the wilderness of their lives on their own. He had even fed them with manna, the food of angels, when they ran out of bread. He humbled them to test them, the scripture says, for one purpose and one purpose only to see if they would keep His commandments; that is, to see if they could reside in their faith in Him.

A definition of faith is "a belief in or confident attitude toward God, involving commitment to His will for one's life" (Thomas Nelson, Publishers). While this is true, it seems woefully inadequate to describe the depth of a believer's hope and trust in the Lord. Perhaps it is impossible to truly define the connection made between God and man through faith, but we can be certain that apart from faith we become wanderer's in a dark and foreboding world without hope for anything beyond the present. But with faith in God, in His Son, Jesus Christ our Lord, and in the power of the Holy Spirit, we acknowledge that which has past, rejoice in the present, and look with anticipation to eternal life in His presence. We repeat; faith is a necessary component of every believer and is vital for his spiritual health.

But the nature of faith, and the love behind it, requires that it also be tested. Every significant character in the Holy Bible had his faith tested. Noah, Abraham, Joseph, Moses, David, Jesus, Peter, Paul and on and on; there are no exclusions. If Adam was to grow and be nurtured in all aspects of human existence while in the garden, he would likewise need to have his faith tested. Faith is like a muscle; it has to be exercised to be strengthened and to remain healthy. The temptation of Adam and the tempting of Jesus served the same purpose—to see if their faith was strong. Jesus passed with flying colors; Adam flunked.

Mankind continues to run up against temptations. In fact, we have become very good at promoting them and entertaining them. As it has been said, "The sin isn't in the tempting, it becomes sin when we entertain the temptation." The history of mankind has proven that we are very weak in resisting temptations even for those of us who proclaim Jesus as our Lord. But it is because of Him and our steadfast relationship with Him that we have hope for redemption, for restoration to a state of righteousness, thereby implanting within us a hope for a return to Eden.

10

PEACEFUL EDEN

So far in our investigation of the makeup of Eden, we have concentrated on plant life due to Genesis 2:9 which we have previously quoted, *"Out of the ground the Lord God made every tree grow that is pleasant to the sight and good for food."* And in chapter 5 we presented evidence that man may have originally been a vegetarian. However, our exploration of Eden and our vision of a return to it has to include the animal world. Add to this God's own statement that *"man does not live by bread alone,"* and we have to consider why God determined to create so many species of mammals, birds, fish, insects, etc.

We first encounter the animal world in Genesis 1:20, the fifth day of creation. *"Then God said, 'Let the waters abound with an abundance of living creatures, and let birds fly above the earth across the face of the firmament of the heavens.'"* And the next day, the sixth day, *"Then God said, 'Let the earth bring forth the living creature according to its kind: cattle and creeping thing and beast of the earth according to its kind, and it was so.'"*

The phrase, *"according to its kind,"* suggests the truth that God created within all creatures the capacity to reproduce themselves. Obviously, it was not God's intent to continue to add numbers to each species; He provided the first pair with all the necessary parts and systems to reproduce, and it was up to them to populate the earth. This is defined in Genesis 1:22 when speaking to the creatures living in the water and the birds of the air, *"And God blessed them, saying, 'Be fruitful and multiply, and fill the waters in the seas, and let the birds multiply on the earth."* It is interesting that the word "blessed" is used here for the first time in scripture, and it refers specifically to this gift of reproductive strength.

Now, reminding the reader of our original premise, that God created the world, the whole universe, for man; we were not an afterthought nor a postscript on creation, but we were God's intent from the beginning; it becomes evident that creation of the animal world, like that of the vegetation, was for the purpose of mankind. Yet we also have to keep in mind that the Eden we are seeking is the pre-fall Eden; before the sin of man resulted in a curse being placed upon the earth.

But what could be the purpose of the immense variety of living creatures, large and small? Why would the Lord God provide such an array which would appear to compete with man, His prized creature, for space and resources? Let's consider Genesis 1:26, "Then God said, *'Let Us make man in Our image, according to Our likeness; let them have dominion over the fish of the sea, over the birds of the air, and over the cattle, over all the earth and over every creeping thing that creeps on the earth.'" And in verse 28, "Then God blessed them and said to them, 'Be fruitful and multiply; fill the earth and subdue it; have dominion over the fish…'"*

This adds a whole other dimension to the relationship of the inhabitants of the earth. Surely, each species had its place; each flock or herd existed within its own order, but with the Lord's charge to man, we learn that the animal kingdom and all of creation would not to be free from the influence of man. The Lord God had given them a manager. To have dominion means to exert control over something; it means to have supreme authority over it. And the word subdue means to "bring into bondage" or to subjugate. This statement also implies that the world in which man was to live was a harsh and wild place which required subduing. This conclusion presents realities which do not always fit within our image of Eden.

As we read the two accounts of creation, we are confronted with questions concerning the placement and role of the animal kingdom. In Genesis 1, it is plainly stated that the fish and the birds appeared on the fifth day, and the four-footed animals, etc. were created on the sixth day just before God formed his crowning glory, man, from the dust of the earth. And there is nothing said about a garden unless we consider verse 30. *"Also, to every beast of the earth, to every bird of the air, and to everything that creeps on the earth, in which there is life, I have given the green herb for food."* Perhaps this is indication of a special place given for these creatures, but it also can describe the whole of the land masses of earth.

However, in Genesis chapter 2, what is commonly called the second account of creation, we find a compressed version God's work, and the sequence of events is not as clear. In this sequence, the forming of man comes first then the planting of the garden of Eden and only later were the animals introduced into it. However, we need be careful not to assume a different and conflicting account of creation, but that chapter 2 only summarizes chapter 1 and adds a description and a name for the neighborhood in which Adam was to live. Most importantly, it defines the rules God set for life in His garden as well as the penalty for breaking these rules. Further, the mention of the animals is in regard to the Lord God having brought them to Adam in order that he should give them names; it does not speak to the timing of their creation.

The fact that God had created a portion of the earth that was outside of Eden also becomes evident; first, in the fact that he created the plants and trees, the grasses and herbs on the third day of creation and later "planted a garden." That is, He set aside a portion of earthly creation as the place where He would dwell with Man and man with Him. This was not the whole of creation but a specific and special part of it.

Second, and more specifically in Genesis 3:23 after Adam and Eve had violated his instruction and warnings about eating the forbidden fruit. It says, *"Therefore the Lord God sent him out of the garden of Eden to till the ground from which he was taken. He drove out the man and He placed cherubim at the east of the garden of Eden...*

to guard the way to the tree of life." Since God exiled Adam to a place outside of Eden and "*to the place from which he had been taken*," Adam had to have been created from the clay which the Lord God had previously created…which was not within Eden.

Also, since God placed a curse on the ground in which Adam was being exiled but not on Eden, (there would be no need to place guards around that being cursed) and there is no mention of God having to create a new home for Adam after the fall. It becomes evident that there was a world outside the boundaries of the garden albeit prior to it being cursed. Even as Adam was living in harmony with God and with all of nature within the garden, there was a world outside the garden which was different. All indications are that it was not idyllic as was Eden; it was a world of conflict and of chaos. It was the world from which Adam had been taken, but it would become the world into which Adam and his seed would return. And it would become a world accursed because of the sin of Adam.

Let's return to our examination of the world God built expressly for Adam to live in, and to which we continue to have a strong desire to return. We have already heard that Adam was most likely a vegetarian, but what about the animals? What about every creature in the sea? The birds of the air and every creeping thing? Everything that crawls, climbs, and slithers? Were they all vegetarian? Were they always in harmony?

We have come to recognize that the world operates within a finely balanced ecosystem. We have come to see how each species from the minute amoeba to the largest mammal are interdependent. Each having its own place and purpose within the broader scope of the earth and for its survival. It is easy to see how worms and earth-dwelling insects and mammals aerate the earth promoting plant life; birds and bees pollenate the plants and aid in their reproduction; larger mammals eat the grasses and return fertilizers to the soils. Animals breath in oxygen and expel carbon dioxide. The plants and trees reverse this process taking in the carbon dioxide and giving off oxygen. This is the basic elementary school version of the science of the ecosystem which in reality is infinitely more complex and totally mind-boggling.

We also have learned much from these creatures that we have been charged to manage. Many exist in social groups depending upon the strength of their numbers for survival. Some show extremely complex team skills as they divide and conquer their work. We have marveled at the wisdom some display in preparing stores of food for dormant seasons and the navigational skills of migratory birds and animals. From the tiniest insect to the immense whales of the sea, the Lord God created them with traits and skills which amaze and even instruct us.

Certain of the animals have become domesticated and help provide for our lives even if we did not eat of their flesh. Cattle, goats, and the like provide milk; sheep give up their wool; fowl produce eggs; and even worms spin webs strong enough to be woven into fine cloth. Horses and similar beasts have become means of transportation and providers of power for tasks too heavy for man while dogs, cats, and some birds have become favored companions and assistants for daily living. Precisely what God had in mind for each, we may never know, but we do know we are to coexist with them.

But the question remains, does co-existence mean total harmony? It is difficult to perceive of an animal kingdom without the checks and balances of a predator/prey confliction. At least, from a perspective of this side of Eden, we can imagine total chaos from the overpopulating of all species left free to reproduce at will. Is it logical that while envisioning the myriad of species to be created, God would have provided a means of population control which could include that one species would be food for another—even in Eden?

The other side of the argument would include the concept of a peaceful Eden. That the Lord God would build within His garden borders the necessary controls to maintain a healthy and idyllic life for all creatures, a place where "the lion would lie down with the lamb." (This, by the way, is not an actual quotation from scripture but perhaps a common misstatement based on the Messianic prophecy of Isaiah 11:6–8, and the end-times prophecy of Isaiah 65:25.) It is comforting to believe that the place God built for man to dwell forever would be totally absent of such agony, even among the least of the species (if there is a least), but does it fit with all the scriptures tell us about Eden.

Let's review what we have learned from Genesis 1 and 2 as there appears to be evidence that all life within Eden was not the perfection of peace. If it were, why would Adam be charged with subduing it and be charged to take dominion over it. Why would his first stated purpose be to "tend the garden." Yes, we can easily understand that the herbs and plants might need some cultivating and pruning. But can we extend such work to the task having dominion over all earthly creatures and of subduing them? Does such language in the scriptures indicate that the natural enmity we see between species today existed in Eden?

Perhaps there is no conclusive answer, and the question has become moot due to the fall of man and our exile from Eden. Yet the desire remains. The forces that pull us back to Eden remain strong. We struggle, understanding that we cannot know the mind of God, yet question how an all-powerful, all knowing, omnipresent God could create an island of perfection within a world seemingly full of chaos and then close the door on it, leaving us outside looking in.

But as radio personality Paul Harvey used to say, "Now for the rest of the story." Fortunately, we have been given to read the remainder of God's story. We know the finish even as its full revelation remains to be exposed. In the meantime, we live on, in a world we were not designed to live, yet not banished from His presence.

Whatever we know about God, and whatever we believe or understand about the story of creation, we can be assured that God knows what He is doing, and that we are blessed to be made in His image and chosen to be stewards of the earth He created.

It seems that God understood that the world left on its own would not remain good or peaceful. It would need to be managed, and it would always have elements within it which were in conflict. The omniscient God would also foresee that sin would enter the world and life would become a struggle. He would know that the creature He had given to manage all He had made would become its chief adversary. Perhaps this was His incentive for Eden. It was to be a model for what life could be. It was to demonstrate perpetual existence in the peace and harmony of living in His presence. And this is sufficient to instill within us a severe case of homesickness for Eden.

11

TAKING COVER

The early parts of this writing deal primarily with the reason God planted the garden of Eden and with the detail provided for us in Genesis chapters one and two concerning the species of trees growing there. At the beginning of chapter 5, we began to speak of other trees; those not identified in Genesis, but which we believe must have been present in the beginning since their fruit relates to the desired character of mankind as expressed in Galatians 5. "Love, joy, peace, patience, kindness, goodness, faithfulness, gentleness, and self-control." At that time, we dropped a hint of a third tree mentioned in Genesis to be discussed later. It is *the fig tree.*

The only way we know the fig tree was growing inside the boundaries of the garden of Eden is that after Adam had sinned against God, he and Eve recognized their nakedness, so they sewed fig leaves together to make a covering for themselves. This makes the fig perhaps the oldest species of tree continuing to exist. Let's consider Genesis 3:7.

> *"Then the eyes of both of them were opened and they knew they were naked; and they sewed fig leaves together and made themselves coverings."* (Some translations say *"Aprons."*)

It is important that we understand the meaning of the words, "Their eyes were opened." It's obvious that Adam and Eve had not been blind in the traditional sense. They surely were able to see all that the Lord God had created for them. We have already learned how Adam responded with joy at the sight of Eve after she had been created. And certainly, they could see as the serpent led them astray by showing them the attractiveness of the forbidden fruit. And as was discussed in chapter 8, there were trees which God provided to be "pleasing to the sight."

But the sentence says, *"Their eyes were opened and they knew their nakedness."* Nakedness means exposure, and exposure of their sin brought shame. This is evidence that their eyes were opened to the truth of what they had done, and for the first time, they experienced the sense of shame. Realizing their sin was about to be discovered by the One they had disobeyed; they tried to cover it up by covering their bodies, at least in part. Listen to the exchange between God and man in verses 8–11.

> *They heard the sound of the Lord walking in the garden in the cool of the day, and Adam and his wife hid themselves from the presence of the Lord God among the trees of the garden. Then the Lord called to Adam and said to him, "Where are you?" So he said, "I heard your voice in the garden, and I was afraid because I was naked; and I hid myself." And He said, "Who told you that you were naked? Have you eaten from the tree of which I commanded you that you should not eat?"*

There is much to consider as we read these few verses of scripture. First, let's consider the pure innocence of the inhabitants of Eden before eating the forbidden fruit. They were in the raw, in the buff, communing with God in peace and tranquility, not knowing shame nor having need to. They existed in the state in which God had created them. Then came the forbidden fruit, the knowledge of good and evil. Immediately they became aware of their nakedness;

evil thoughts entered their minds. The sin of lust entered their hearts and minds and became active in their lives, and they were ashamed. In chapter 3, we discussed at length the effects the tree of the knowledge of good and evil had on humanity. In this case, the maxim, "ignorance is bliss" certainly holds true. Once the knowledge of evil entered man's mind, it poisoned his soul and condemned our person forever—except for God's love and His great capacity for mercy.

As soon as Adam confessed his nakedness, God knew what they had done. *"Who told you that you were naked?"* was not only his question but the conviction of His words. *"Have you eaten from the tree I told you not to eat?"* God already knew the answer.

Most of us, at some time, have done something for which we were immediately ashamed? Perhaps this act came by accident or as the result of a decision which seemed right at the time, but God brought conviction to our heart? There was a fear rising in us. "How can I correct this? I am so ashamed. How can I cover up what I have done?" were the kinds of thoughts that raced through our minds. Confession and atonement are the only answers, but these eluded Adam. We will get back to this later, but first, let's learn a bit from the fig tree.

The fact that they chose the leaves from this tree may be a matter of convenience as much as anything else. The leaves had to be large enough and tough enough to be sewn together to form a covering for these sinners. They had to cover their sensitive parts. But the tree also produces fruit—tasty fruit. There are numerous varieties of figs with differences in appearance and growth patterns, some depending on the climate and the soil conditions, etc. A fig tree can be little more than a large shrub if growing in poor soil, but may be a large tree where sufficient nutrients are present. Having been planted in Eden, we can assume the fig trees available to Adam were large healthy trees. And healthy trees are covered with large healthy leaves.

Since the fruit of this tree became a major food crop and object of commerce in later days, we assume it would have been a favorite of Adam as well. In addition to being his major source of sugars, figs provide an array of vitamins, minerals, and natural fiber which would have been good for his general health. Adam would have stayed close to these trees and enjoyed them immensely.

Fig trees are mentioned numerous times in both the Old and New Testaments. Often this tree was used as an indicator of prosperity as in Deuteronomy 8:8 when the bounty of the promised land is spoken and in 1 Kings 4:25 in describing the prosperity of Solomon's reign.

> *"Every man will dwell in safety under his own vine and his own fig tree."*

The inverse of this is also true as the absence of the fig was deemed to be an indicator of God's judgment on the land and on the peoples.

> *All the hosts of heaven shall be dissolved, and the heavens shall be rolled up as a scroll; all their hosts shall fall down as the leaf falls from the vine and as fruit falls from a fig tree.* (Isa. 34:4)

> *He has laid waste my vine, and ruined my fig tree; He has stripped it bare and thrown it away; its branches are made white.* (Joel 1:7)

These verses and others like them give testimony to the value of the fig. Seen as a blessing when it is plentiful; a curse when it is taken away.

Such a curse is found in the New Testament as gospel writers Matthew and Mark speak of an incident in which Jesus cursed a tree because it was not bearing fruit. This is a curious story in that it seems to be out of character for Jesus to show anger at an inanimate item, and it is even more so as Mark reveals that it wasn't even the season for figs (Mark 11:13). But Jesus never does anything without a reason.

Both chroniclers of this story indicate that Jesus saw this tree from far off and saw that it had leaves. Knowing that it wasn't the season for figs, Jesus immediately saw the opportunity for a teaching moment. A feature of the fig tree is that it blooms before its leaves come on, and the fruit begins to develop as the leaves are growing. Therefore, any person of that region, seeing a fig tree with leaves, would have assumed it should also be bearing fruit. So Jesus cursed this tree, and it immediately dried up—end of story, right?

Not quite, while it is easy to identify a reference to the problem of the Pharisee, a healthy outward appearance while bearing no fruit, there is more to learn from this incident. Listen to Matthew 21:20–22.

> *When the disciples saw that the tree was withered, they marveled, saying, "How did the tree wither away so soon?" So, Jesus answered and said to them, "Assuredly, I say to you, if you have faith and do not doubt, you will not only do what was done to the fig tree, but also if you say to this mountain, 'Be removed and be cast into the sea,' it will be done. And whatever things you ask in prayer, believing you will receive."*

To understand the message Jesus was teaching, it will help to understand the setting in which it was spoken. Jesus had the previous day entered Jerusalem with great acclamation; the whole city was excited about his arrival and were hailing Him as King of the Jews. Then He had entered the temple and drove out the money-changers, and those He called a "*den of thieves.*" Now having returned to Bethany for the night, he had awakened and was preparing to go back into Jerusalem. (By the way, the name Bethany means *House of unripe figs.)*

Biblical historians have traced Jesus's steps and believed that at this moment, He and his followers were standing on the Mount of Olives looking to the west where not only could they see most of Jerusalem but also Herod's palace, and by turning their focus to the south, far in the distance was visible a shining sliver of the reflected light coming off the Dead Sea. Herod's palace sat atop a mountain he had increased in height by cutting the top off an adjacent hill and using the rock and dirt to build the foundation for his palace. This, in an apparent effort to prove that he had the power to build mountains—the power of God. It is possible that the demonstration Jesus had embarked on was intended to encourage his followers to keep believing in Him. Knowing what was ahead for them, He was encouraging his disciples to stand firm in their faith, that if they prayed and believed even that mountain on which sat the despised Governor of Judea would be cast into that distant sea; the sea which at that time was often used as a repository for remnants of pagan temples and other things profane.

While this story does not directly relate to the fig tree in the garden of Eden, it is a prime example of the importance of this tree, and of the many ways, it has impacted the history of our Judeo-Christian faith. Another example is found in Luke and Matthew as they relate a parable Jesus taught in response to inquiries about the end of the age. Jesus reminded them that when they see the fig tree in bloom, they know summer is near, but even as the end of the age is as sure as summer is coming, they will not know the day nor the hour until it is upon them.

And speaking of the End of the Age, we would be remiss if we did not include John's mention of the fig tree in Revelation 6:13. The fig trees of Israel bear twice each year; the second, "late" or "winter" crop is subject to the harsh weather and often beset by winds, etc. which cause them to fall to the ground. In the vision John saw of the Lamb opening the seven seals on the scroll of judgment and redemption of which only He was worthy to loosen, the sixth seal was opened with the vision.

> *I looked when He opened the sixth seal, and behold, there was a great earthquake; and the sun became black as sackcloth of hair, and the moon became like blood. And all the stars of the heaven fell to the earth, as a fig tree drops its late figs when it is shaken by a mighty wind.* (Rev. 6:12–13)

The message is that when Christ returns at the end of the age, these great cosmic events will seem to come as easily as the fig tree loses its winter crop in a strong wind. All of the power of the universe will be unleashed culminating in the end of the reign of evil on the earth.

We have included some of the biblical history involving fig trees to indicate their intrinsic value to mankind from the beginning to the end of life on earth, and even as the brief history we are given of Adam in the garden, the impact of this tree extends far beyond the fact he used it in a futile attempt at covering his sin. The extent of his futility can be seen as we learn what God does next.

We know that there is a consequence to sin—a severe penalty.

> *For when you were slaves of sin, you were free in regard to righteousness. What fruit did you have then in the things of which you are now ashamed? For the end of those things is death. But now having been set free from sin, and having become slaves of God, you have your fruit to holiness, and the end, everlasting life. For the wages of sin is death, but the gift of God is eternal life in Christ Jesus our Lord.* (Rom. 6:20–23)

This passage not only testifies to the consequence of sin but defines the remedy God called forth in Jesus Christ. We will get back to this later; but for now, let's continue with our examination of the immediate effects Adam's sin had on him.

Having learned of Adam's sin, we hear in Genesis 3 the specific consequences God pronounced on the serpent, on Eve, and on Adam. For our purposes, we will concentrate on Adam.

> *Then to Adam, He said, "Because you have heeded the voice of your wife, and have eaten of the tree of which I commanded you, saying, 'You shall not eat of it:' Cursed is the ground for your sake.* (or because of you*) In toil you shall eat of it all the days*

> *of your life. Both thorns and thistles it shall bring forth for you and you shall eat the herb of the field. In the sweat of your face you shall eat bread till you return to the ground, for out of it you were taken; for dust you are, and to dust you shall return.*

Even as the curse God spoke was on the ground, its effects on man are major. Instead of living in a lush garden where everything he would need, everything that was pleasing to the eye and good for food, was at his fingertips, it literally was his for the taking; he would now have to work hard for it. He would have to contend with every sort of evil the earth could throw at him. He would have to work for the rest of his life.

Even more serious were the statements indicating, he was now mortal; death was a certainty for him.

> *"In the sweat of your face you shall eat bread till you return to the ground, for out of it you were taken; for dust you are, and to dust you shall return"* (Gen. 3:19).

Compare this sequence with that of Genesis 2:7.

> *"And the Lord God formed man of the dust of the ground, and breathed into his nostrils the breath of life; and man became a living being."*

To make man, God used the substance of the earth—the same dirt that would produce the plants he would eat, sustain the garden in which he would dwell, and house all the animal world who were to be his companions. But after the fall, after Adam sinned against God, he would return to his original state, to the earth. *"To dust you are, to dust you will return."* What is missing in this statement? It is the breath of God; the life-giving spirit that God breathed into him. He would return to the same state he was before God scooped him up and breathed life into him. There can be no doubt that God had pronounced a death sentence on Adam and his descendants. The wages of sin is death!

There was one last interaction between God and Adam before he banished him from the garden.

> *Also for Adam and his wife the Lord God made tunics of skin, and clothed them. Then the Lord God said, "Behold, the man has become like one of Us, to know good and evil. And now, lest he put out his hand and take also from the tree of life, and eat, and live forever" — therefore the Lord God sent him out of the garden of Eden to till the ground from which he was taken. So He drove out the man; and He placed cherubim at the east of the garden of Eden, and a flaming sword which turned every way to guard the way to the tree of life.* (Gen. 3:21–24)

This could very well have been the end of the story. The man God had created in His own image had violated His trust and flagrantly disobeyed his one restriction for life in His presence. It wasn't just that God was angry with this man, but He could not risk the eternal consequence if man would now eat of the tree of life; the prospect that sin itself would become immortal. The solution was to banish him from the garden and make sure that there was no chance that he would ever eat of the tree of life. Death would have to become a part of his living experience.

Yet in this same passage of scripture we find that the love God has for man could not be turned off. In a great show of compassion and mercy, God looked upon this pathetic creature now clothed in shame and trying to hide behind an apron of fig leaves. If the situation had not been so serious, we may have found the Lord God doubled over with laughter at the ludicrous picture Adam presented. Just imagine the scene; here stood the man God had deemed to be "king of the jungle" as it were, now standing with head bowed in shame trying to hide from God the Father and creator of all, using only a few leaves borrowed from a tree—all-in-all, a pathetic picture.

God looked upon this sorry sight and said, "This won't do. We can't turn this man loose in the world with no more covering than this." So he fashioned tunics for both of them out of animal skins. And where did the skins come from? An animal had to give up its life. There had to be a sacrifice. Blood had to be shed to cover the sin of Adam. This was the first sacrifice for sin, and it was the model for many more to come.

There are numerous references for sin offerings comprised of animal sacrifice—the shedding of blood as atonement for sin in both the Old and New Testament but mostly in the Old. In Exodus 29:14, we find instructions to Moses and Aaron requiring a sacrifice of a bull as a sin offering, and Leviticus 4 provides detailed instructions given to Moses from the Lord God for the offering of animal sacrifices as sin offerings. For our purposes, we will acknowledge that God provided the original sacrifice to cover Adam's sin. Yet even this did not move him into a state of eternal life.

Another Old Testament story involving animal sacrifice is in Genesis 22 when God tests Abraham's faith by instructing him to sacrifice his only son, the son of the promise, on an altar of fire. When Isaac asks his father, *"Where is the lamb for a burnt offering?"* Abraham's answer, *"My son, God will provide for Himself the lamb for a burnt offering."* And after Abraham believed on God and prepared to sacrifice Isaac, God did reveal the lamb he had provided for that sacrifice. Just as in a later time, He would reveal the Lamb, His own Son, as the sacrifice sufficient to redeem the lives of those who would believe in Him.

The writer of Hebrews uses this incident along with many others from biblical history to show how the faith of the believer is counted as righteousness in God's eye. We trust that we don't have to recount the mount of biblical evidence that, after centuries of animal sacrifices, God declared it was not burnt offerings and the sprinkling of an animal's blood that he desired, but that men would repent of their sins and turn their hearts to Him. His desire was for man to be obedient in all his ways; the same requirement He had made of Adam as He sat him down in God's own garden.

Hebrews 11:8, *"By faith Abraham obeyed when he was called to go out to the place which he would receive as his inheritance, not knowing where he was going."* Verse 17, *"By faith Abraham, when he was tested, offered up Isaac, and he who had received the promises offered up his only begotten son, of who it was said, 'In Isaac your seed shall be called,' concluding that God was able to raise him up, even from the dead."* Then as James wrote, quoting from Genesis 15, from God's covenant with Abraham to make him the father of nations. *"And the Scripture was fulfilled which says, 'Abraham believed God, and it was accounted to him for righteousness.'"*

The point is made that Adam, having been convicted of his sin tried to cover it up; he used fig leaves in an effort to hide from the Lord. But God, even as he had to punish Adam for his disobedience, even as He had to separate him from the tree of life, said in essence, "Fig leaves aren't going to cut it. I have a better covering for your sin. It involves sacrifice."

The fig tree may have been planted to provide for man's physical need for the nourishment of his body; and Adam may have seen in it a place to hide, but Adam's feeble attempt at covering his sin actually provided an excellent opportunity for God to demonstrate His love, His grace, and mercy. Adam may not have considered being evicted from his home as anything but totally bad news, yet within the bad news, the Lord provided a ray of hope. He provided a remedy for sin—the shedding of blood which only He could provide.

The fig tree has no direct impact on God's ultimate solution for the sin of man, but it provides a very good reminder of how inadequate we are when left to our own devices and how feeble our efforts when we try to handle the consequence of our sin without God. The fig may be a very good symbol of God's provision when approached with an attitude of praise and thanksgiving. But it also can telegraph a weakness in our spirits, a failure to trust the Lord.

12

Life with a Purpose

"Man's chief aim is to glorify God
and enjoy Him forever."
—Westminster Shorter
Catechism, 1647

Life is more than breathing and eating. One of the strong desires of mankind is to know that we have a purpose; we want to know that our being here makes a difference, and that in doing so, we have been pleasing to someone other than ourselves. So far, we have dealt seriously with the physical requirements of human life, and in the discussions regarding the gifts of the Spirit, we have covered some of the more tangible aspects of life—those things which might be considered as character traits. But what does God have to say about the purpose of man?

In the course of this writing, we have already discussed several factors pointing to God's purpose in creating man, but let's refresh our memories a bit. First of all, we should acknowledge that man is God's crowning achievement of creation. We alone are created to be in his image, and God decreed that man have dominion over all other of His creation (Gen. 1:26). However, it must be stated that having dominion does not mean having our way with what belongs to God. It means ruling as God would rule. It places on mankind the responsibility to grow, foster, protect, and wisely use the things of the earth.

Indeed, the first thing God did for man after creating him and breathing life into him was to bless him and to charge him with populating the earth. *"Then God blessed them and said to them, 'Be fruitful and multiply; fill the earth and subdue it'"* (Gen. 1:28a). Of prime importance to our question as to the purpose of man is the fact that God breathed life into him. All other living beings began their lives upon God's word. He spoke, and it was true. But God chose for man not only to be made in his likeness, but that He breathed life into him. More than just commanding that we breathe the air around us, God breathed His breath into us. He gave us the substance that made Him a living Lord. That is, He infused us with our moral, intellectual, relational, and spiritual capacities. He gave us the stuff of His character including the capacity to resist Satan.

In Genesis 1:28, we find the word "subdue." *"Fill the earth and subdue it."* The words used here actually means "to bring into bondage." Perhaps we could say, "Fill the earth and make it work for you." The world God created for mankind was not to be his enemy; it was not to present unconquerable challenges. It was not to beat man down, but man was to live in it, respect it, and use it to accomplish the things God had ordered for him.

Consider Genesis 2:15. *"Then the Lord God took the man and put him the garden of Eden to tend and keep it."* Add this to his commands—to fill and subdue—indicates that the Lord God had work for man to do; he had a purpose. The Eden God provided was perfect. It was the ideal environment created specifically for man to dwell, yet it required that man, *"Tend and keep it."* We know that physical and mental activity are necessary for us to maintain healthy bodies and minds, and it seems that God designed this into us from the very beginning. It was part of His original intent and is prime for us to acquire a sense of purpose and self-worth.

We find this yet today as a man's identity and self-worth is often wrapped up in his work. But as we have learned from Genesis 3, the story of man's failure to trust God, work outside the garden confronts a myriad of problems unknown to the inhabitants of Eden. After the fall of man, God removed him from Eden and placed him outside, where "thorns and thistles" abound, and the work became arduous, "*In the sweat of your face you shall eat bread.*" Where in Eden, food was no further away than low hanging fruit and work was a pleasurable occupation; outside, a man would have to toil just to put food on his table, and his work would be exhausting to both body and soul.

We will consider life outside the garden a little later, but let us return to the grand design of God, to the place God built specifically to house the joy of His heart. Of all the reasons we can find relating to the purpose of our creation, none is more important than the fact that we were made to be companions of God. We were made to walk with Him and talk with Him. We were made to be in His presence to enjoy Him, and for Him to enjoy us. Throughout this book, we have used the traditional translation of God's words of introduction to the concept of man, "*Let us make man in Our image.*" However, scholars have taken a second look at this phrase in the ancient documents and have concluded that it can also be translated as "Let us make man as Our image." This is an important distinction because it provides a better, or perhaps a more complete understanding of the mind of God and of His motivation for creating us.

Throughout scripture, we find evidence that God instructed mankind, or that man was inspired to leave memorials at specific places of importance during their life's journey. They were to be as memorials to remind folks of where they had come and to teach the next generations the importance of their walk with the Lord and especially of the places of their interaction with God. If we apply this kind of thought to the phrase, "*Let us make man as our image*," we begin to understand why the Westminster shorter catechism declares, "Man's chief aim is to glorify God, etc."

God is spirit. He is invisible to mortal man. Being the image of God places upon us the responsibility to demonstrate the character of God and become as memorials—as living reminders of His presence with us and in us. If we could see ourselves as a memorial to God as well as His companion, we might strive a bit more to be like Him—that is to be in and *as* His likeness.

So how do we glorify God? First, we glorify Him when we trust Him. We give Him glory by our obedience and by the way we conduct our lives. Saint Paul writing to the Church at Ephesus said,

> *In Him* (Christ) *also we have obtained an inheritance, being predestined according to the purpose of Him who works all things according to the counsel of His will, that we who first trusted in Christ, should be to the praise of His glory. In Him you who also trusted, after you heard the word of truth, the gospel of your salvation; in whom also, having believed, you were sealed with the Holy Spirit of promise, who is the guarantee of your inheritance until the redemption of the purchased possession, to the praise of His glory.* (Eph. 1:11–13)

And in 1 Corinthians 10:31–11:1,

> *Therefore, whether you eat or drink, or whatever you do, do all to the glory of God. Give no offense, either to the Jews or to the Greeks or to the church of God, just as I also please all men in all things, not seeking my own profit, but the profit of many, that they may be saved. Imitate me as I imitate Christ.*

(More about giving glory to God in chapter 8.)

There is ample evidence in scripture of our need to give glory to God but often the purpose of such actions eludes us. God is not some exalted egomaniac demanding that we acknowledge Him continuously. Instead, the act of giving glory to God demonstrates that we understand who God is and who we are in relation to Him. When we find ourselves in the presence of the all-knowing, all-powerful, ever-present God; when we understand that he is Creator, sustainer, provider, protector, Savior, companion, and friend, it is difficult not to give Him glory.

A weak example from our lives might be when we have met our soulmate; when we have found the person we love so much that we can hardly stand being away from them, even for a moment; when we see everything in them as perfect and nothing they do can detract from our love for them, we can't help but tell everyone we know, even some we have just met and perhaps perfect strangers, of how great this person is.

Giving glory to God isn't a commandment as much as it is the only reasonable response to His presence in our lives. Giving glory to God doesn't elevate God (He is already exalted above all others); it elevates us. It reinforces in us the power of His image, that which He gave us the moment He breathed life into us. In a way, each moment spent in giving glory to God exercises our awareness of who we are in the Lord thereby strengthening and renewing our spirits.

Imagine for a moment, (hopefully it is more a memory than a conjured-up image for you); a loving father or mother is watching their small child play along a creek bank. Almost with every step, there is a new discovery, a new adventure, and they squeal with delight at each flower, with each colorful stone, with learning how to pick up a crawfish or feel the squirming worm they found in the grass. With each new discovery, they come running to show mom or dad what they have found. And the parent finds they are having as much fun as the child as they watch him enjoying the world they have shown him. This is the way God receives the glory we give Him as a loving Father who loves to see His children enjoy all that He has provided for them. But the real beneficiary is the child who discovers how great it is to be a companion of God.

Often our understanding of giving glory to God is framed by our church activity, specifically in our worship experiences. Far too often, we become so preoccupied with the process of making a living and doing the things our world tells us is pleasurable that we all but forget God. To overcome this, we establish a regimen of weekly worship, maybe an hour or two on Sunday, perhaps a midweek service, and for others, a daily regimen of prayer. This is all good, but in reality, it doesn't always give glory to God.

Giving glory is an act of worship, one which is intended to be continuous. We are to live our lives as worship to God, and we do this by striving to remain as His likeness and in demonstrating who He is through our words and actions. But Christ tells us that there is acceptable worship, thus also implying our potential for unacceptable worship.

In the *story of Jesus meeting the Samaritan woman at the well, he tells her,*

> *"The hour is coming, and now is, when true worshipers will worship the Father in spirit and in truth; for the Father is seeking such to worship Him"* (John 4:23).

Also in Genesis 4 is the story of Adam and Eve's first two sons, Cain and Abel.

> *"In the process of time it came to pass that Cain brought an offering of the fruit if the ground to the Lord. Abel also brought of the firstborn of his flock and of their fat. And the Lord respected Abel and his offering, but he did not respect Cain"* (Gen. 4:3–4)

Abel offered the first and the best of what God had given him. He made a sacrifice to God; indicated by mentioning the fat of the lamb. Apparently, Cain's offering did not meet these qualifications and God rejected it. As Jesus would later say to the woman at the well, *"True worshipers will worship in spirit and in truth."* That is, they will have *hearts for worship;* they will return to God the tithe that is due Him, and they will do it with honesty and humility. All this is an act of worship; it is giving glory to God through grateful praise and thanksgiving for all He has given us.

There are other aspects of acceptable worship such as confession of sin, praying, hearing, and responding to the world of God, etc.; not all of which were necessary in Eden. A great image of the Church and its earliest worship comes from Acts 2 beginning at verse 42.

> *They continued steadfastly in the apostle's doctrine and fellowship, in the breaking of bread, and in the prayers. Then fear (reverence) came upon every soul, and many wonders and signs were done through the apostles. Now all who believed were together, and had all things in common, and sold their possessions and goods, and divided them among all, as anyone had need. So, continuing daily with one accord in the temple, and in breaking bread from house to house, they ate their food with gladness and simplicity of heart, praising God and having favor with all the people. And the Lord added to the church daily those who were being saved.*

So if the chief aim of man begins with giving glory to God. We have learned it begins when we become the kind of people He designed us to be, those who are *as* His image. The image best demonstrated as we are able to worship Him in spirit and in truth.

The second part of the Westminster short catechism states that we are to enjoy Him forever. This seems easy enough. After all, we all love the Lord our God, right? However, the examples of our lives say this isn't so. The history of mankind shows that we disobey Him, try to hide from Him, run from Him, become afraid of Him, deny Him, disrespect Him, distort His word, and generally ignore Him. All such acts we find in the Bible, and all are prevalent in our society today.

The truth is, we can't enjoy what we don't know, and we won't know what we believe has no relevance in our lives. Earlier in this work, we commented that even as God had evicted man from Eden, He had not given up on man. Yet in many ways and to varying degrees mankind has turned his back on God.

In Revelation 22, beginning at verse 2, as John relates the details of his vision of the New Jerusalem,

> *He showed me a pure river of water of life, clear as crystal, proceeding from the throne of God and of the Lamb. In the middle of its street and*

> *on either side of the river was the tree of life which bore twelve fruits, each tree yielding its fruit every month. The leaves of the tree were for the healing of nations. And there shall be no more curse...*

This is so reminiscent of the tree of life planted in the middle of the garden of Eden and calls us to remember the curse God spoke upon the earth as he evicted Adam and Eve, the curse which was the result of their sin and which included the sentence of death. In the New Jerusalem, in the presence of God and the Lamb, the curse has been lifted; all sin has been erased; and there is no death. The earth as we have known it will have passed away; a new heaven and a new earth will have been lifted up, one without a curse upon it (Rev. 21:1).

This, Revelation 22, is a comforting scripture. It is the hope that keeps believers going, for it speaks to the future dimension of "Forever." However, there is also the now. As it is said, "He (Jesus) was in the beginning, is now and will be forever." And if we are to understand the Gospels, our participation in the future depends greatly on the preparation we make in the present. And that preparation begins when we say, "Yes" to Jesus. It begins when we enter into relationship with the Lord.

Jesus has told us that the gateway to heaven opens for us when we believe in Him. *"I am the way, the truth, and the life, No one comes to the Father except through Me"* (John 14:6). He is the way to the Father; He has opened the door; He has restored the line of communication with God the Father; He has made it possible for us to once again walk with Him and talk with Him as our first parents did in Eden.

But every relationship requires mutual respect, commonality of purpose, and a union of love. And not only has Jesus made that possible, He sent the Holy Spirit to enable and empower us to operate in this relationship.

We have lived a long time in an alien world, a world not designed for us. We have tried to possess it, subdue it, and change it. Instead, it appears as if we have disfigured it, polluted it, overpopulated it, and all but destroyed it. And somehow, we still believe that we deserve to live in a future world of perfection. Fortunately for us, God has chosen not to give us what we truly deserve but sent us a Savior He called His son, Jesus.

And through all these thousands of years, the Lord God has allowed us to maintain a memory of the place He originally prepared for man to live, a place called Eden. As we have seen, Eden was special. It was special because it was prepared especially for man, the creature He made to be special. Read on and see if your primordial memory includes a vision for a return to Eden.

13

Homeward Bound

Jesus looked out from the cross and saw the crowd which had gathered to watch Him die. Some were grieving; some trying to hide so as not to be identified as being among His followers. Others cheered and/or jeered at him. Still others just stood with mouths open trying to take in the horror of what they were seeing, not wanting to be there but finding it impossible to leave.

Then He heard a voice and turned his head toward one of the two thieves who were being crucified at the same time albeit for far different reasons.

> *"Lord, remember me when You come into Your kingdom,"* this man had said. Jesus responded, *"Assuredly, I say to you, Today, you will be with Me in Paradise"* (Luke 23:42–43).

There is much to understand from this passage, not the least of which is the thief's statement of faith in Jesus, calling him Lord and acknowledging the authority of His kingdom. Of equal importance is that Jesus received this man as a repentant sinner and assured him that salvation was immediate. *"Today you will be with Me."* The impact of this statement and its importance to our understanding of the grace of God cannot be overstated.

However, of prime importance to our subject is Jesus's declaration of the place they were to share—*paradise.* This is a word used sparingly in scripture. In the New King James Version of the Bible, it is used only three times and each time referring to either Eden or heaven.

The word *paradise* comes from a Persian word meaning a wooded park or garden. It often was used to define a walled park of fruit trees, what we would call an orchard. All-in-all, an apt description of our image of Eden. Both the Greek and the Hebrew words translated as Eden in the Old Testament mean blessed. Primarily, it is used to indicate *the blessing of being in the presence of God.* Even today, the expression "Eden-like" refers to a place of perfection, that which is idyllic in appearance and character and which exists in perfect harmony—i.e. heaven!

The story of the thieves on the cross identify two basic types of people in our world—those who will look at the evidence that Jesus is Lord and believe and those who will see the same evidence but stubbornly cling to their unbelief. The really difficult thing for us to understand is that Jesus loves both. The one He can save; the other He has to let go. In one, He rejoices; the other remains a source of grief.

Scholars, archeologists, etc. have spent hundreds of hours and days, even lifetimes, researching and searching for the location of Eden. Some believe it exists in what was once known as Persia, specifically the area between the Euphrates and Tigris rivers. Others think it refers to the entire Fertile Crescent from Persia to Egypt. Others still propose that it is in North Africa where scientist chasing DNA evidence have determined to be the origins of human existence. But we propose that Eden exists wherever man lives in perfect harmony with God.

Let's review what we know. God is Spirit. Man is made in the image of God and with the expressed intent that he lives in the presence of God. Therefore, he possesses the ability to live in this spiritual realm. The book of the Revelation of Jesus Christ begins with the declaration that John, the receiver of the revelation, was "*in the Spirit* on the Lord's day" when he heard the voice of the Lord (Rev. 1:10). The testimony of John confesses that he was having a spiritual encounter with the Lord; he was having an "out-of-body experience." The invitation and teaching of Jesus is for us to become more like Him, i.e. to live more in the spiritual.

Earlier, we presented biblical evidence that of the "food" found growing in the garden of Eden were those which later would be described by Saint Paul in his writing to the Galatians as "Fruit of the Spirit." We argue that if these today are the fruit, or result, of living in the Spirit, then they were readily available in Eden to sustain man as he existed within the spiritual presence of God and grew in his relationship with the Lord. That is, what we receive from the fruits of the Spirit in Galatians 5 are the nutrients we need to grow and maintain a healthy spiritual relationship with the Lord. Apples, pears, and bananas are food for the body. Love, joy, peace, etc., are food for the soul.

We also have learned from our study of Genesis 1 through 3 that mankind, Adam and Eve, were not at first aware of their bodily presence. It wasn't until they had eaten the forbidden fruit that "*their eyes were opened and they saw their nakedness.*" This could also be stated as they existed in a perfect spiritual dimension with God their father (who is Spirit) until the time they disobeyed Him and ate from the tree of the knowledge of good and evil. Having eaten this forbidden fruit, they became aware of their nakedness. That is, they became aware of their physical and now mortal bodies.

At this same time, having become aware of the sin of His prized creation and understanding the full ramification of it, God had no choice; He could no longer allow mortal man to live in Eden, in Paradise, which is a place for those pure in spirit. So He banned him to a mortal existence in a world which He also cursed so as to impress upon this man the consequence of his actions. However, we state again, that while God separated himself from man, He did not abandon him. The Old Testament is a history of the Lord's continuing interaction with man and His numerous attempts to persuade us to return to Him, to re-establish a relationship with Him.

This might be a good time to discuss another passage of scripture which is often overlooked in the study of Genesis.

> *Then the Lord God said, "Behold, the man has become like one of Us, to know good and evil. And now, lest he put out his hand and take also of the tree of life, and eat, and live forever"—Therefore the Lord God sent him out of the garden of Eden to till the ground from which he was taken. So, He drove out the man; and placed cherubim at the east of the garden of Eden, and a flaming sword which turned every way to guard the way to the tree of life.* (Gen. 3:22–24)

It is the latter part of this passage in which we invite your attention. God had exiled Adam to a life which had a beginning and an end; it was a harsh and uninviting place. Very quickly, Adam may have turned around, screaming, "I don't like it out here. Let me back in!" But God had taken preventive measures to assure that Adam could never return to the garden of Eden.

God clearly stated His reasoning, *"Lest he put out his hand and take also of the tree of life, and eat, and live forever."* Having tasted sin, having eaten of the forbidden fruit, God could not allow this fallen man to become immortal, not while in this state, so He had to prevent him from sneaking back in. The fact that God did not destroy man at that time—It would have been easy. There were only two of them—says that God already had a plan for the redemption of man, a plan which once again provides hope for access to paradise.

So God installed a two-part barrier to guard the tree of life, cherubim and a flaming sword. Artists and biblical commentators often portray the cherubim as a warrior angel holding and waving the flaming sword. But nowhere does the scripture say this. Such images may make sense to those of us who know that objects like swords need someone or something to make them move and do the work for which they were intended. But let's examine what the scripture really says.

First of all, "cherubim" is the plural form of the word cherub. A cherub is a spiritual being; one of the Lord's angels created before the creation of the earth. As spiritual beings, even as they may take on a bodily presence as the task requires, they operate freely in God's spiritual realm. If God placed "cherubim" at the east of the garden, there was more than one cherub.

Secondly, the scripture does not say the cherub or cherubim was waving the sword, nor does it indicate they were in the same spot. Perhaps this is splitting hairs, but the cherubim were placed at the east of the garden and the flaming sword was put in position to guard the way to tree of life which was in the midst of the garden. Granted, this could mean the cherubim and flaming sword were in the same location, but it seems to indicate they were separated as two different ramparts in a common defense system.

The issue isn't so much the placement of the cherubim and the sword but the sword itself. Those familiar with the Hebrew texts state that the verb translated as "turned every way" can mean "turning itself" as being self-animated. It denotes an active and dangerous presence. At the same time, nearly every biblical scholar agrees that this flaming sword is representative of God's judgment and is a powerful statement concerning the separation of God and man as the result of Adam's disobedience. The bottom line is that God had passed judgement on Adam for his sin and created an impenetrable barrier to assure that he would never return to Eden.

Earlier, we made reference to the use of the names Eden and Paradise as being synonymous. They refer to a place of special peace and comfort, a place of happiness and blessedness in the company of the Lord God. The Septuagint, the ancient Greek translation of the Old Testament uses the word *Paradeisos* for the garden of Eden in Genesis 2:8, and we find the same word is used in the three New Testament references to heaven meaning a place of future peace and happiness—an eternal Eden. And in both, man is pleased to dwell with the Lord and He with them.

Therefore, it is germane to our topic that we consider the relationship between Eden and heaven. For sure, there are many similarities between what we know about Eden and what we understand about heaven. We are presented with rivers flowing out of Eden and from the Throne of God in heaven. We are told that a *tree of life* is present in both, and in both, we are introduced to a life of perfect peace in the presence of God. Consider the following:

The tree of life is found in both Eden and heaven. Genesis 2:9, "*And out of the ground the Lord God made every tree grow that is pleasant to the sight and good for food. The tree of life was also in the midst of the garden...*" Compare this to Revelation 22:2, the description of the New Jerusalem in heaven. "*In the middle of its street, and on either side of the river, was the tree of life, which bore twelve fruits.*" The tree of life in both cases symbolize eternal life. In Eden, this tree was in the middle of the Garden and out of this garden flowed the river which branched into four major rivers sufficient to sustain life for the world. In the New Jerusalem, the river flows out from the Throne of God, and the tree of life is in the middle of that stream. Both in Eden and in heaven, the tree of life is positioned such that it is sucking up the waters of life flowing from the presence of God. And the tree of life is in the middle; it is the center of God's presence. "*I am the living water,*" says the Lord. "*If anyone thirsts, let him come to Me and drink. He who believes in Me, as the Scripture has said, out of his heart will flow rivers of living water*" (John 7:37–38).

Another level of comparison can be made between Genesis 2:12 as it describes Eden with the words, "*And the gold of that land is good, Bdellium and the onyx stone are there.*" And Revelation 21:19–21 describing the numerous jewels and precious stones which make up the Holy City culminating in verse 21 with, "*The twelve gates were twelve pearls: each individual gate was of one pearl, and the street of the city was pure gold.*" Here again, we find a common description between Eden and heaven; and in 1 Peter, we are told these precious stones represent the true believers who make up the body of Christ, His church. "*Coming to Him as living stone, rejected indeed by men, but chosen by God and precious, you also, as living stones, are being built up a spiritual house, a holy priesthood, to offer up spiritual sacrifices acceptable to God through Jesus Christ*" (1 Pet. 2:4–5). In the description of the New Jerusalem in Revelation, the precious stones of heaven become more valuable the closer they get to the throne of God. Likewise, the precious stones we represent become more refined the closer we get to the Lord our God.

Next, let's consider the other tree that was in the garden of Eden, the one conspicuously absent from heaven, the tree of the knowledge of good and evil. We have already discussed the nature of this tree and considered the reason the Lord God even planted it in Eden. By now, we should surely understand the consequence of Adam and Eve having listened to the serpent and eaten of that tree. And chief among the consequences was man's exile from Eden and the curse that was placed upon the earth because of him. "*Cursed is the ground for your sake; in toil you shall eat of it all the days of your life*" (Gen. 3:17b).

Because Adam and Eve hung their hopes and their future on this tree of the knowledge of good and evil instead of the tree of life, the sentence of hanging from a tree is seen as a curse; it was the ugliest form of execution and usually reserved for the vilest of criminals. *"For he who is hanged is accursed of God"* (Deut. 21:23b). At that time, hanging did not mean that a person was hanged by the neck until dead, but that a person killed for their crimes by stoning and beating was hung for public display for one day. Similar practice had been carried forward to the time of the Roman occupation of Israel and was the reason the enemies of Christ called for Him to be beaten and crucified, to label him among the worst of those deserving death, and to display Him as an example to any others who might want to proclaim themselves to be God.

But when Christ overcame this sentence of death by rising from the grave, He reversed this curse. He showed that righteousness, His righteousness, was more powerful than the curse and lifted it for all who turn to Him. Saint Paul said it well in Galatians 3:13, *"Christ has redeemed us from the curse of the law, have become a curse for us [for it is written, 'Cursed is everyone who hangs on a tree']."* The tree, of course being the cross of Christ. Saint Peter used similar language as he said, *"He, himself bore our sins in His own body on the tree, that we, having died to sins, might live for righteousness"* (1 Pet. 3:24).

What we have presented is evidence that the curse God placed on man and upon the earth as He exiled Adam from Eden was removed and does not exist in heaven. But also, we have learned that the means by which it was removed came by way of a third tree of life—that which is the cross of Christ. It was not for sheer poetry that Saint Peter, when defending his preaching the gospel of Jesus Christ in public, stood before the High Priest and declared, *"We ought to obey God rather than men. The God of our fathers raised up Jesus whom you murdered by hanging on a tree"* (Acts 5:30).

The Bible, while being contained in one volume, provides a history of the life of man and of his relationship with His God from the first thoughts of God to a description of life eternal. In between, we see the struggles of man, struggles born out of disobedience and its result, exile from Eden, being banned from the home which the Lord God designed in His mind and built with His hands for the expressed purpose of living with His prized of creation. Yet the end of the story tells of a reunion; the reuniting of the faithful believer and God in a new home He has prepared for us to live forever. If we were to take an in-depth look at biblical history and attempt to make a diagram of mankind's route from Eden to heaven, it would be quite circuitous. But it can also be simplified and perhaps more understandable if we see it as a straight line from Eden to heaven and passing through Calvary.

Earlier, we asked the question if Eden and heaven were one and the same, and the answer was no. But we have to conclude that Eden was very much like heaven in that it was a place of harmony, a place where man dwelt in a close relationship with God and a place where he had the opportunity to eat of the tree of life and thus fulfill God's hope for him, that he would live forever. Yet what we see of heaven is even greater. Not only physically and visually better, but spiritually because there is no more sin.

> *Now I saw a new heaven and a new earth, for the first heaven and the first earth had passed away… And I heard a loud voice from heaven saying, "Behold, the tabernacle of God is with men, and He will dwell with them, and they shall be his people. God Himself will be with them and be their*

> *God. And God will wipe away every tear from their eyes; there shall be no more death, nor sorrow, nor crying. There shall be no more pain, for the former things have passed away."* (Rev. 21:1, 3–4)

This is infinitely better than even Eden before the fall. Perfect life, eternal life in the presence and for the purpose of "glorifying God and enjoying Him forever" (Westminster Shorter Catechism).

So Eden isn't heaven, and we are not being given an opportunity to return to Adam's homeland. Instead, heaven is a new Eden, restoring that which is most important to God, including His desire that his prized of creation be given a new opportunity for eternal life.

We began this journey by stating that we have this primordial memory of Eden; it was implanted within us at the beginning in the seed which has been propagated through Adam and Eve and all generations which have followed. And this memory causes us to be homesick; we long to return to our roots. But as we have searched through God's word and probed the hearts and minds of key figures in the Lord's story, we have discovered that our primordial memory hasn't taken us back to Eden but caused us to look forward to the New Eden, the New Jerusalem and a renewed and forever life in the presence of God.

At the same time, this process has allowed us to discover, or to have reinforced in us, the fact that the object of our search, the conditions we have longed for aren't so far away as we have thought. The conditions we identified in Eden to some degree remain available to us yet today. All of the desirable traits we find in Galatians 5 love, joy, peace, patience, kindness, goodness, faithfulness, gentleness, and self- control remain with us as gifts of the Holy Spirit. The gift of faith is ever present, as it is the power given by the spirit to enable us to believe and to proclaim, "Jesus is Lord." Those things pleasing to the eye are all around us and are most evident when we discover the beauty of the Lord and give glory to His name. The tree of life we have found in the work of Christ upon the Cross. And yes, we are still confronted by the tree of the knowledge of good and evil, and it remains for us, forbidden fruit.

In this world today, we are constantly faced by the need to make a choice, the same choice that our fathers and their fathers before them have had to make, to choose good or choose evil, to choose life or to choose death, to follow the Lord Jesus Christ or to reject Him. The good news is that we have the Holy Spirit in us to help us.

For sure, in our present state, in the world in which we remain in exile, we are far from paradise and will not reach that level of perfection promised in heaven, but we can get a lot closer than we are. We have a longing within us to return to Eden. We have a hope within us to get to heaven. Both goals simply mean we want to live in the presence of God; we want to be his friend and companion. And He desires the same of us!

Perhaps when you were a child, your mother baked a cake, and you begged to be able to lick the bowl, to taste of the cake you knew would come. It was not the cake, but it contained all its sweetness; it had not risen to perfection, yet you could envision its completion. You had to wait, but being allowed to taste the batter and to smell its aroma as it baked only heightened your anticipation and expectation of what would come. Such is life in the promise of God and the presence of the Holy Spirit.

Let's return for a moment to Revelation 2:1–7. This is Christ's instructions for a letter to the church at Ephesus reminding them to return to their first love. He is asking them to return to the Lord their God. "Give Him your all." He says, "Let all you do, all you say, all your thoughts flow out of your love for Him and from the knowledge of how much He has loved you." To understand this, perhaps it would be good to take a moment to tear apart verse 7.

"*He who has an ear, let him hear what the Spirit says to the churches.*" This refers to the believers whom the Spirit has given the wisdom to understand. *"To him who overcomes,"* to the one who perseveres in obedience in spite of persecutions, temptations, etc., "*I will give to eat of the tree of life.*" Note that it is *a gift* given by Jesus; a gift delivered from the cross. Who will eat of the tree of life? He who overcomes the world. See first John 5:4–5, *"For whatever is born of God overcomes the world. And this is the victory that has overcome the world—our faith. Who is he who overcomes the world, but he who believes that Jesus is the Son of God."*

To summarize, we began life in a perfect spiritual relationship with God, one that was designed to be eternal. Because of our disobedience and the sin of pride (believing that we could be like God), we were exiled to a world not our own. In it, we have existed for thousands of years; an imperfect human existence which includes the reality of death. Now, we are given the opportunity to return to a perfect spiritual and eternal relationship with the Lord. And all it takes is for us to follow the instructions which God first gave to Adam. "Eat of all the trees in the garden, except do not eat of the tree of the knowledge of good and evil. Do not pursue the forbidden in lieu of that which leads to eternal life."

Our beginnings were in Eden; our hope is in heaven. The bridge between them is the cross of Christ.

About the Author

After a lifetime of being a nominal Christian, Dale Minor experienced a move of the Holy Spirit upon him which eventually led to stepping aside from a responsible secular position (Vice President, Engineering for a privately-owned Plastics Injection Molding Co.) to help start a new church and then to seminary after which he was ordained its priest and pastor. This congregation, established in Circleville, Ohio, affiliated with the Anglican Church in North America with the mission of reaching souls for Christ incorporating the three streams of worship expression, The Evangelical, Pentecostal, and Sacramental-Liturgical. After eighteen years of serving that congregation, the author moved to Meigs County, Ohio, to be closer to family and to serve his new rural Appalachian Community. Writing has long been an avocation of Pastor Minor's expressed through numerous newsletter articles and through what he calls E-Musings; weekly e-mailed commentaries on life and the holy scriptures. In 2018, he published his first book, *His Familiar Voice,* a testimony of learning to know the powerful and beautiful voice of God.